MIDNIGHT ARCADE

Fantastic Fist / MowTown

by Gabe Soria
art by Kendall Hale

Penguin Workshop

DIRECTIONS

One thing you'll learn quickly here is that it's not always easy to follow the instructions. You never know when the game . . . I mean, book . . . is going to send you to your doom. But if you want a truly exhilarating experience, you'll need to do exactly what the book tells you . . . except, of course, when you get to make a choice. In these cases, you should trust your gut.

When you see a game controller like the one below, you'll be presented with multiple options to move around or take an action. Once you make a choice, turn to the corresponding page and find the matching symbol.

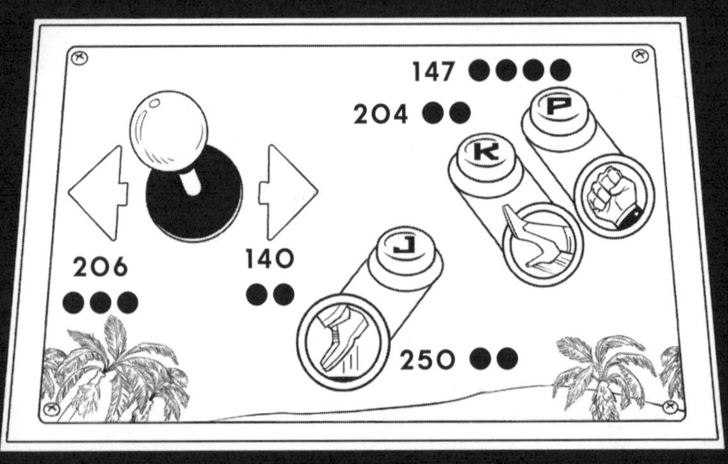

There can be as many as four sections on a page, so make sure you ONLY read the one marked with your symbol for that page.

At times, you'll be sent to a page and symbol without a choice or be presented with a chance to return to the previous stage. Do as you're instructed to keep the story flowing correctly.

Sometimes you'll make a wrong choice, and the game will end. At that time, you'll have a choice to either restart that level or exit the Midnight Arcade.

There are countless ways to read this book . . . I mean, play these games . . . I mean, read this book . . . I mean . . . Well, you get the picture. Have fun, and good luck!

Welcome to the MIDNIGHT ARCADE

As the express train you're on speeds past stations and rattles toward its mysterious destination, you think back on the events of the past few hours that have led you to where you are now, on your way to the last stop of a strange subway line in the big city . . .

You didn't tell anybody that you were skipping school today, so nobody knows about your plan: to take a train into the city and explore all day. You don't know why, but you feel like something was calling you there today; it was a mysterious feeling, but an urgent one, so you decided to throw caution to the wind and heed it and say whatever to your perfect attendance record.

When you got dropped off at school, you successfully snuck around back and then slipped away down an adjacent street, carefully avoiding the prying eyes of curious adults wondering why a kid like you would be wandering around during a weekday. Soon, you made it to your town's suburban train station and purchased a ticket for the 7:58 a.m. for the city. Minutes later, the train pulled up and you boarded, found an empty seat, pulled out the sandwich that was meant for your lunch, and began to munch.

After arriving at the city's central train station, you found a map of its subway system. Inspecting it thoroughly, you eliminated lines to ride and potential destinations until you arrived at a decision: the MA line seemed to go the farthest out, and to a neighborhood designated on the map as "Arcadia," which you liked the sound of. Decision made, you found the transfer point and caught the next train.

But that's when the weird stuff began to happen. Or, rather, that's when you started to actually NOTICE the weird stuff. First off, the car you boarded was practically deserted. The only other passengers were solitary, and they got off one by one at the first few stops until you were the only person still on board. At the stops after those, no one else got on. Then, the speakers in the car crackled, and a voice that sounded like a teenage dude playing a prank rang out, a little too loudly.

"This train is now express to Arcadia. Hang on to your hats, folks!"

The train switched gears (do trains do that?) and began to accelerate faster and faster, rocking back and forth and passing stations by at a speed that HAD to be unsafe. You were going so fast that you could barely make out the faces of the people standing on the platforms. The brakes squealed whenever you hit a corner, but the train never slowed down TOO much. Sparks flew up from the wheels, illuminating the dark subway tunnel with flashes of light, but still the train kept going . . . and going . . . and going. It might have been express, but it sure seemed like a LOOOOOONG way to your destination. And that's where you are now, hoping that the train eventually slows down before it crashes.

Almost as if in answer to your thought, the train surprisingly begins to slow down, and the speaker comes alive again.

"Next stop, Arcadia," says the same goofy voice as before. Moments later, the train pulls into a station and then—THUNK!–comes to a complete stop. The doors open with a hiss and stay open, and the hydraulics let out a sigh of steam.

The speaker crackles. "This is the end of the MA line, and this train is now out of service. Please exit and make sure you take all of your belongings with you." You can almost swear you heard the announcer giggle at the end of the announcement. Figuring that you have no choice in the matter, you grab your backpack and leave the car.

It doesn't look like a popular stop. The station's platform is dirty and grimy, the way a place gets when it's in a state of perpetual neglect and disuse. But the

WALLS of the station itself are pretty rad. You've heard about artists being commissioned to make art for different train stations in the city. This is definitely one of those installations. The name of the stop, Arcadia, is spelled out in tiled letters that look like the title text from an old video game, and the little illustrations in the other decorative tiles look like sprites from that kind of game, some that you think you recognize (is that a character from *Excellent Ernesto Cousins* over there?), but most are unfamiliar.

Pretty cool, you think as you walk past them. And as you move, you catch another detail: The tile sprites seem to have been made and placed so that if you blink rapidly as you walk, they "move" in limited animation cycles, roughly approximating the look of old arcade games. It's a strange but neat effect. Someone spent a lot of time placing the tiles just so, and you decide to revise your opinion: *Very cool*, you think.

It makes it even more surprising to you how such a cool station can be so empty. This place has surely been written about on one of those cool websites that document interesting but obscure places.

Finally, you come to the end of the platform and, pushing your way through a turnstile and passing a long-abandoned attendant's booth, you ascend a set of stairs that leads you to the streets of Arcadia.

You can sense that there's something decidedly strange about this place the moment you come out from the underground, for the bright morning you left when you first descended into the subway has somehow, in the space of a subway ride (how long were you on that train, anyway?), turned into night. But you push that strange detail aside almost immediately, so enthralled are you by the exciting vibe of the neighborhood. Arcadia is a riot of color and confusion; neon lights blink in the windows of noodle shops, cool and strange music pumps from stereos, bikes and cars jockey for space on its streets, and people from seemingly everywhere crowd its sidewalks, dressed in an incredible variety of clothes and speaking dozens of different languages. There's no doubt about it: Arcadia is RAD.

You begin to wander the twisting streets of the neighborhood, reveling in the feeling of freedom in your exotic surroundings. Everything around you is new, fascinating—the sights, the sounds, the smells—and soon you're lost in the maze of the neighborhood and, looking around, you realize that you have no idea how to get back to the subway station.

And that's when you hear something, a familiar something: the tinny, lo-fi, utterly unique sound of vintage video game sound effects! You look around, peering at the shops around you, trying to locate the source of the noise, and that's when you see it: a basement storefront, just ahead of you below street level and accessible by a set of concrete stairs. You approach the stairs cautiously, a little reluctant to descend, but after a moment's hesitation, you figure what the heck and go down. The place doesn't have a sign, and you can make out only blinking lights shining through its dirty windows, but the sound of games is louder down here, so you reach for the door handle. Taking a breath and swallowing your fear, you pull the door open and walk in . . .

. . . and find yourself in what appears to be a dimly lit maze of arcade cabinets, the screen of each one glowing with power. Their speakers are the source of the sounds you heard from the street, and bunched together in this low-ceilinged, cramped room, the hundreds of different games produce music and sound effects that combine into a cacophonous, but not unpleasant, avant-garde digital symphony.

You begin to wander the aisles, and before long you're deep in the strange room. It's bigger on the inside than it looked on the outside, and after minutes of wandering, you still haven't come to any of what should be its walls. It's as if this basement storefront were connected to every other basement on the block. Ignoring this, you focus on your surroundings: games of every genre and description are crammed into the space, from fighting games to imported dancing challenges to weird UFO catchers offering prizes from animated shows you've never heard of (*What's a "MegaGhost"?* you wonder). There's even a booth that promises a "chess-playing chicken," but sadly, the chicken seems to be hiding in its coop or to have moved on.

Then you pass by an encouraging sight—a change machine, meant to take bills and convert them into coins to allow you to play games. Unfortunately, the slot you'd slide paper money into is taped over and won't take the dollar you've pulled from your pocket. You don't have any quarters on you and you're worried you won't get to play any of these awesome games. Frustrated, you give the machine a gentle pound with your fist and the jostling seems to have an effect, for something rumbles within and a stream of gold coins empties into the change machine's small catch basin. Not believing your luck, you grab some of the coins and inspect them. They're unlike any coin you've ever seen before.

Holding the handful of coins, you feel . . . something, something you can't quite put your finger on, but something special all the same. You slip most of the coins into your pocket but keep one grasped firmly between your thumb and forefinger. It's time to play a game.

"Ahem!" You hear a throat clearing dramatically behind you, and you spin around, clutching your token and ready to flee. Standing before you is a young man with shoulder-length hair, wearing ratty jeans, an old-fashioned coin-changing belt, and a long-sleeve T-shirt. He smirks, and you notice that there's something . . . odd about his eyes, as in, THEY'RE KIND OF GLOWING. Scared, you begin to haltingly offer an apology for trespassing and offer him the token. He shakes his head and waves you off.

"Hey, no worries about that. You figured out the way to get some freebie tokens; they're yours. That's how things work here."

Here? Where's here? Is he implying that the law of the land in this arcade is "Free games for everyone"?

"Read the shirt!" he says, and you notice that the logo for a place called the Midnight Arcade is emblazoned across the front. "That's right, you've found the Midnight Arcade, the most primo game palace in this or any other dimension. And since you've scored a token, that means you get to play. Killer, huh?"

Without noticing, you've been backing up, away from this strange arcade attendant, only stopping when you bump into something solid. Turning, you see that you've come to a cul-de-sac in the Midnight Arcade, a dead end occupied by two games. Unlike the other games, they are turned diagonally to face each other. It seems obvious that they have been selected for you.

"Oh, yeah! These are two of the raddest games in the whole place. You show excellent taste, my friend." You take a step back and take in the scene. To your surprise, the attendant now stands between the two game cabinets, his lanky arms open in a gesture inviting you to play. On one side of him is a game called *MowTown*, and its cabinet art depicts what looks like a fairly hectic day of lawn mowing, with a variety of strange obstacles and opponents. On his other side is a game called *Fantastic Fist*, which seems to be mostly about a very strong person using their fists (ah!) and other handy items to cut a swath through a steady stream of increasingly outlandish opponents. They both look pretty fun, and you could swear that the token in your hand is actually getting warmer, as if the proximity to these games has awoken something inside of it. But that's impossible.

"That's actually NOT impossible," says the attendant with a grin, seemingly reading your thoughts. He points at your hand. "That token wants to play a game. But how about you? You ready to get down and go for a high score?"

You consider the attendant's words for a moment and then nod. You've come all this way and have some free tokens, so it would be a waste to leave without at least checking out some of the games, right? Right! You step forward and glance from game to game, your token at the ready. Which one will you play first?

If you want to play *Fantastic Fist*, head to 185 ●●●●

If you want to play *MowTown*, head to 192 ●●●●

●

Realizing that you can't do anything without the Mow-Luxe running, you grab the machine's cord and pull. HARD. The engine comes to life once again, and its noise makes the snake retreat, but only slightly.

Head to 92 ●

●●

Your lasers can't seem to find the tiny target quickly enough, giving him time to complete his sequence. A fireball erupts in front of the chopper, and you fly straight into it, unable to react in time. You know what that means? That means that . . .

YOU ARE DEAD. CONTINUE: Y/N?

Y: Head back to 203 ●● N: Head to 248 ●●

As the topiary creatures charge, you leap up into the air, landing on the rock that, until moments ago, was the home of the Golden Clippers. You've bought yourself a few precious seconds, but your next choice is critical. Choose again . . . and choose wisely!

Head back to 144 ●●

Disarmed, Pistolwhip stills stands defiantly between you and the chopper. "I'm just as deadly with this as I am with a whip," she shouts, brandishing her laser pistol at you. "For R.A.T.!" she adds, and then she fires! You barely have time to react.

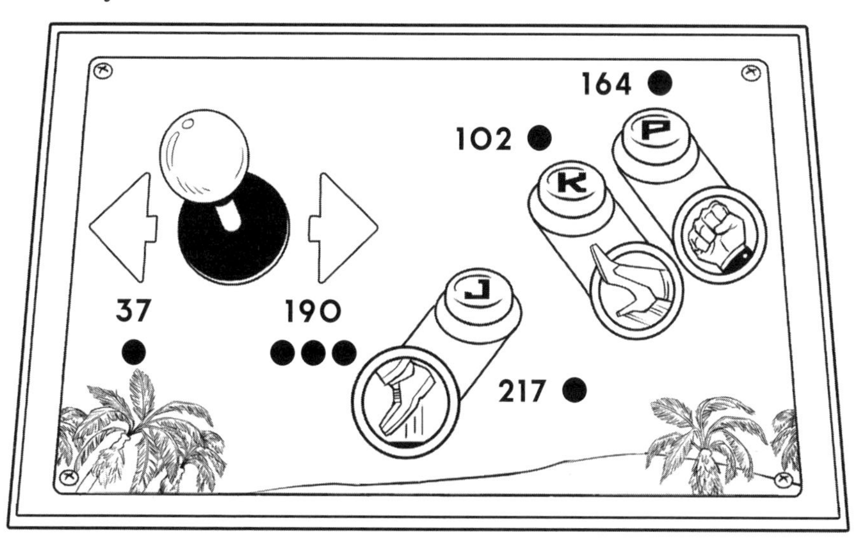

You nod. He approaches you and gestures for you to follow him out of the room and back to the hallway. You trail him as he walks farther down the hall, toward what looks to be Vineland's back door.

"That you found the Golden Hedge Clippers shows that you are a bold and adventurous sort, the type that doesn't simply follow the easy path. That kind of sauce is essential in both life AND gardening. Excellent! Now go forth, young one. Go forth into the Garden of Battle, and may the spirit of summer fill your soul and inspire you to victory over the vines."

Having reached the end of the hallway, the Ancient Gardener throws open the great glass doors that lead out to the backyard of Vineland.

Descending a set of stairs, you finally settle on a vast plain of grass that extends hundreds of yards in all directions. Ringed by well-kept hedges, and with strange symbols cut into its beautifully maintained grass, it's nothing less than the ULTIMATE LAWN, a swath of grass that any groundskeeper would be proud to maintain. You kneel and run your hand over the smooth blades, marveling at the artistry involved in keeping it so neat, and the motion of your hand sends a shiver across the top of the greenery. You watch in wonder as the small disturbance from your touch fans out, spreading and growing, until by the time it reaches the far side of the yard, it's a wave. When it hits the hedge at the far end, another shock wave bounces back, the force of which knocks you backward.

And that's when you hear it: what sounds like an entire forest being crunched, folded, and sawed and made into . . . something. Something mighty, but something wrong. Getting up, you see a form begin to emerge from over the garden wall, a massive beast made not of flesh, but of leaf and vine and branch, all of its body parts clipped into terrifying shapes through the Ancient Gardener's strange horticultural magic. Stepping into what you now realize is a massive arena in which to duel is . . .

TOPIASAURUS REX!

The monster before you is a three-headed towering titan of topiary, a creature from your worst horticultural nightmares . . . but also kinda COOL-looking, too. It looms over you and looks down at you. There's no mistaking it: This creature wants to drive you into the ground and plant you deep. The beast sways for a moment, looking for an opening, and then charges with surprising speed! What's your move?

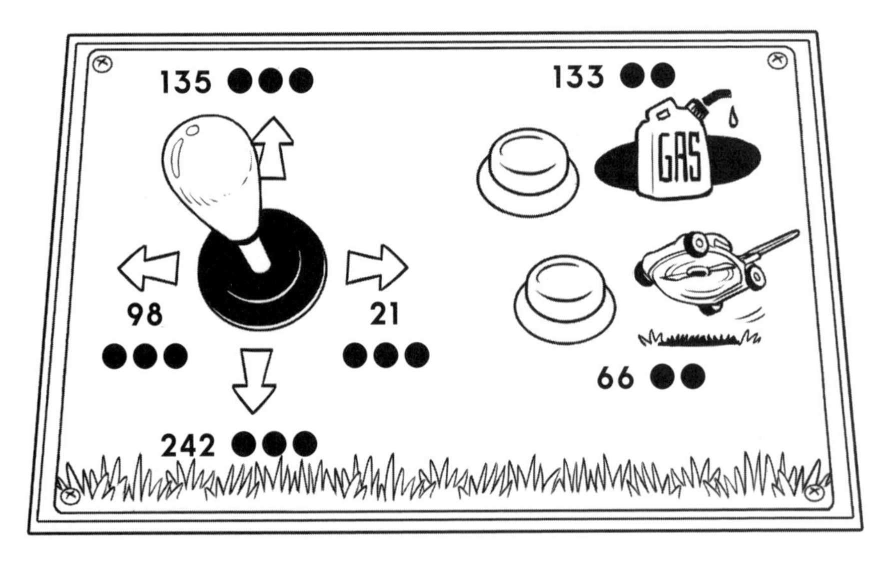

●●

Wait, you actually chose to wait and see? That's not a serious option. That's a joke, kid. A put-on, a gag. You're trapped in a video game, not participating in your school's Model UN as Switzerland. *Fantastic Fist* is a side-scrolling brawler (that's a game where you fight) about kicking butt in creative ways, all held together with a loose plot. It's not about diplomacy. Sheesh! But hey—it's the thought that counts. Your heart's in the right place. That said, go back to where you just came from and choose again.

Head back to 106 ●

●●●

You jump off the King Snake Crawler, which gives King Snake time to press the button and not only re-spawn Pistolwhip and Dobermann Pincer from the R.A.T. Hole but also to repair his vehicle. King Snake presses another button, which sends a shock through the surface of the King Snake Crawler that you definitely want to be sure to avoid in the future.

Head back to 216 ●●●●

You grasp the mower's handlebar, and immediately you feel . . . powerful, like you're holding a magic sword in a fantasy kingdom, only in this case the magic sword is a souped-up lawn mower and the fantasy kingdom is a delightful suburb. At any rate, your garage door is open, you're facing the outside world, and a vision appears to you: the controls on the *MowTown* machine back in the Midnight Arcade.

You realize that you'll have to think like you're playing the game to progress. So: Where do you want to mow, er, go?

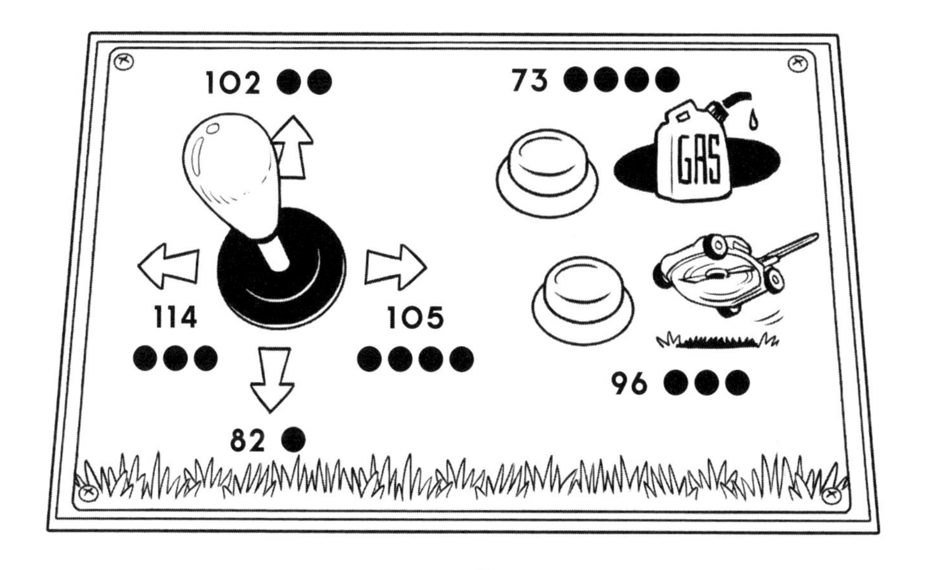

●

You creep back a little and find that you've come to the edge of the cliff and you can't just jump off of it. The only way to go is forward into the fight! Choose again.

Head back to 18 ●●

Leaving Old Lady Olsen's house, you jog through the suburban streets of Lawndon, pushing the Mow-Luxe before you and passing the general hubbub of lawn-mowing activity. Groups of kids working on yards point and whisper when you pass, and you can hear some of their words over the noise of push mowers and internal combustion engines.

" . . . beat the Hedgelordz. Can you believe it?"

" . . . going up to Lawndon Acres . . ."

" . . . Old Lady Olsen's yard—wow!"

" . . . gonna meet Murray up there . . ."

Soon, you leave the orderly streets of suburbia and cross into a section of town that looks more exclusive and wealthy. The road starts winding, and eventually you pass a sign that points up a hill and indicates that

Lawndon Acres Country Club is up just a little farther. Minutes later, a guard booth appears on the side of the drive. A wooden traffic arm blocks it, and a stone wall with spikes on top extends in each direction on both sides of the road. A sign arches overhead:

You approach the booth and see a security guard sitting inside, dozing off as he attempts to read a newspaper. Squinting, you can see its title—*The MowTown Messenger*—and when you clear your throat to get his attention, he startles awake, dropping his reading material.

"Whuzzat, who's there?" he says, blinking at you. He looks you up and down, skeptically taking in your grass-stained attire and the Mow-Luxe. "You aren't a member here, are ya? Nah, you must be that hotshot new lawn-mowing kid making all the news down there in town." With that, he picks up his newspaper and jabs a finger at a picture on the front page—it's a picture of you underneath a headline that reads "Hotshot New Lawn-Mowing Kid Makes News!"

The guard pushes a button on a console in his booth, and the traffic arm rises. "Well, keep on going up the hill until you reach the Shed," he says. "That's where the groundskeepers keep all their stuff. You'll get briefed on the job there. And, kid—good luck with this joint."

As you push the Mow-Luxe through the gate, he adds, "You're gonna need it."

❖❖❖

Soon, you arrive at the Shed, a well-kept garage sitting

in a remote location on the vast estate of the Lawndon Acres Country Club. Outside the Shed's large open doors stands an older man wearing loud checkered pants and a brightly colored polo shirt. Nearby, a group of preppy teenagers are sitting on fancy riding lawn mowers, all of them wearing matching sunglasses and polo shirts tucked into belted shorts. They must have a psychic connection based on being snotty, for all of them sneer at you in disdain simultaneously. Upon spotting you, the older man rushes over, waving a golf club frantically.

"You're here. Finally!" You recognize his voice as belonging to the man you talked to on the phone. He grabs your hand and shakes it rapidly. "Glad to meetcha, kid. You come highly recommended. Old Lady Olsen doesn't vouch for just anybody, you know."

"I told you we could do the job, Uncle Rodney," says one of the preppy kids. You can see now that each of their riding lawn mowers has the words "The Rakes" painted on the side in fancy, looping script.

"You be quiet, Kirk! This situation is your fault in the first place. You and your hoity-toity flunkies. Sheesh!" Rodney, the older man, bugs his eyes out at you and mutters under his breath, "These born-rich kids, I'm telling ya . . ." He shakes his head in disbelief. "So you think you can handle it?" Before you can even ask WHAT you'll be handling, Rodney shakes your hand again. "Sure ya can! I'll leave it to you. Start cutting!"

Rodney stalks off in the direction of Lawndon Acres' clubhouse. As he passes his nephew and the other Rakes, he snaps his fingers, and they follow him on their mowers. But as they do, Kirk, their leader, gives you one last dirty look, flips his long bangs with a flick of his fingers, and pops his shirt collar. What the heck is going on here?

Suddenly you hear a noise coming from somewhere far down the country club's golf course, maybe near the eighth hole. It sounds like the roar of a lion combined with the cry of . . . well, you don't know. Whatever it is, it sounds scary.

"That's Murray," croaks a voice from the Shed. Looking over, you see that it belongs to what appears to be a mechanic, judging from the grease stains on his hands and clothes, standing at the Shed's doors. "You think your job is just to cut the grass for their golf tournament this afternoon? Nope. HE'S the real job," he says, turning his back and disappearing into the darkness of the Shed.

That was strange. Who—or what—is "Murray"? And

what does it have to do with cutting the golf greens at a country club?

If you push the Mow-Luxe toward the sound of "Murray," head to 212 ●

If you go into the Shed to investigate, head to 201 ●

Hand in hand, you push off from the surface of the bridge . . . directly into the path of the giant Cyberanha, whose momentum pushes you off your path over the edge! As you fall, it continues to chomp its razor-sharp teeth at you. In fact, those are ACTUAL RAZOR BLADES you're seeing—those R.A.T. research scientists are some really creatively twisted people. The spectacle is so fascinating yet disturbing that you don't even notice the rocks below rapidly rising to meet you.

YOU ARE DEAD. CONTINUE: Y/N?

Y: Head to 84 ● N: Head to 248 ●●

●●●●

You see that there's a button on the dashboard of the Grass Yacht that looks a little bit like the throttle on your Mow-Luxe, so you reach out to press it and see what it does. Before you can, the Mechanic grabs your wrist and says, "Be careful with that, kid. Only use that button when you absolutely have to. It's too dangerous to use here in the Shed. For now, do something else."

Head back to 201 ●

●

The R.A.T.'s enthusiasm is no match for your training, and you wait until the last second and then unleash the fury of your fist on his flunky face, sending him flying past the pilot and crashing through the windshield. The pilot turns and looks at you, and deciding to join the fight, she leaves her seat. But she forgets to put on the autopilot! The craft lurches, and you lose your footing and tumble through the open door!

Head to 94 ●●●●

●●

You push the Mow-Luxe forward, but remember too late that the engine isn't running! Not only do you not cut any of Ms. Olsen's grass, the snake slithers forward and rapidly wraps itself around you, squeezing you tight and opening its fanged mouth wider . . . wider . . . wider . . . ugh. Sorry. We can't look. Let's just assume that . . .

YOU ARE DEAD. CONTINUE: Y/N?

Y: Head back to 95 ● N: Head to 248 ●●

●●●

You advance on the R.A.T. henchman with menace in your eyes, and he suddenly seems a little less confident. Time to go on the attack and choose another move.

Head back to 18 ●●

●●●●

As Topiasaurus Rex lunges toward your position, you jump, land on its remaining head, and jump off again. Confused, the creature looks around and comes in for a new attack, catching you off guard after your graceful dismount, and strikes!

YOU ARE DEAD. CONTINUE: Y/N?

Y: Head to 170 ●● N: Head to 248 ●●

●

The Ancient Gardener shakes his head sadly.

"You have no hope against Topiasaurus Rex if you haven't found the Golden Hedge Clippers. I'm sorry, but I can't send you into battle so unprepared."

He waves his hand, and suddenly the sound of a thousand lawn mowers fills the room. It's so loud that you put your hands over your ears and shut your eyes, hoping to block out the deafening roar. Then, as quickly as it began, the sound stops. You open your eyes and . . .

Head back to 39 ●●

●●

In the air above the crowd appears a flashing digital title that reads:

And then it disappears. Aw, yeah! You get it—*Fantastic Fist* is a side-scrolling brawler. You flash back to the controls on the *Fantastic Fist* cabinet, thinking that if you're going to get through this, the best way to do it would be to think of it like a game:

All right, all right—enough strategizing and research. It's time to FIGHT!

You start sprinting in the direction that Captain Lu went, toward the parking lot and his helicopter, but before you've even made it to the front row of seats, your way is blocked by a soldier of R.A.T., who wields what looks to be some sort of massive crowbar—and beyond him, there is a mass of more thugs, each one of THEM carrying a crowbar. What, can't R.A.T. afford to equip their flunkies with laser pistols or electric whips or something, you don't know, a little more lethal? What a stingy international order of evil . . .

You're trying to get to the chopper, but your way is blocked by a R.A.T. henchman. "You gotta get through me, jerk!" he says, somewhat unnecessarily. What's your move?

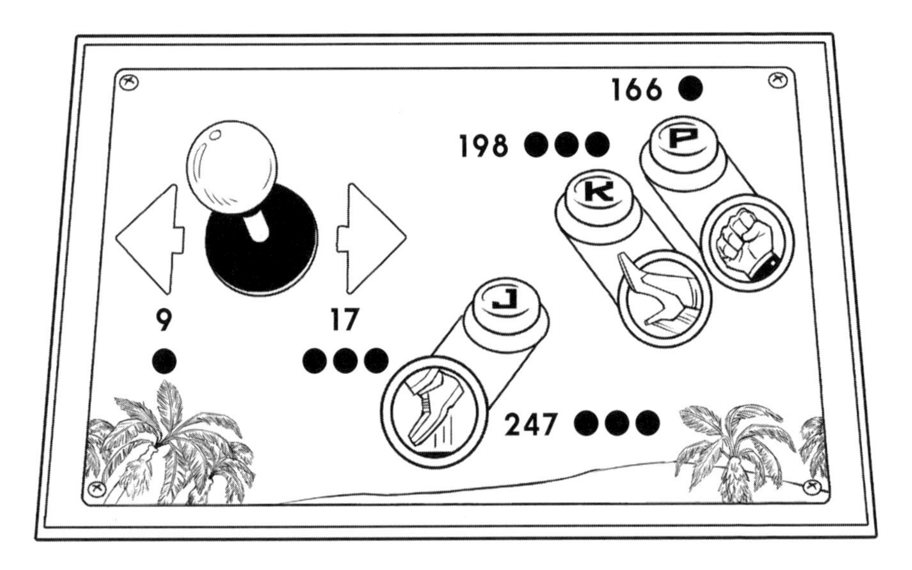

●●●

Topiasaurus Rex is almost upon you, and you zag to the right just as it thunders past, shaking the earth and almost knocking you to the ground. You manage to stay on your feet, but the monster is turning around for another charge. Choose again!

Head back to 3 ●

The Fantastic Fist is almost completely charged up from the last use. Almost! A few more moments and you'll be able to use it again. Just time it right! But now, do another move!

Head back to 237 ●

●

You're not going to retreat. You're not going to dodge. No, you came to Vineland to clip some hedges. Topiasaurus Rex's head snakes toward you, and at the last nanosecond you step aside, bringing the Golden Clippers together around its neck, severing the branches and separating hedge head from hedge body. YEAH!

Head to 53 ●●●●

●●

You kick, but the R.A.T. flunky sidesteps it and then sweeps your leg with a kick of his own, causing you to tumble out of the helicopter's open door! You desperately try to grab the chopper's landing skids, but you're so surprised that you just fall, fall, fall down into the ocean below. Tough break on your wedding day.

YOU ARE DEAD. CONTINUE: Y/N?

Y: Head to 106 ● N: Head to 248 ●●

You push the Mow-Luxe forward, determined to meet this subterranean menace head-on, but right before you hit the furrow in the earth, something explodes from beneath you, sending you and the Mow-Luxe flying and covering you in dirt. Looking up, you see the thing that was down there.

It's Murray.

And it's . . . whoa.

And you? Well . . .

YOU ARE DEAD. CONTINUE: Y/N?

Y: Head to 10 ●● N: Head to 248 ●●

You leap into the air as Pistolwhip moves in for the attack, clearing her head by barely an inch as she passes underneath. You circle each other until you're back in your original positions. Move again!

Head back to 195 ●

●

The Grass Yacht hops into the air, aimed directly at Murray's head . . . uh, actually, to be more accurate, you're aimed directly at Murray's open mouth—in particular his very cute, very big, very sharp teeth—which chomp down on you with excellent timing. Yes, it's true . . .

YOU ARE DEAD. CONTINUE: Y/N?

Y: Head to 115 ●●●● N: Head to 248 ●●

You kick Dobermann when he's down, flipping him over onto his face. Cold-blooded but pretty funny. Make a new move!

Head back to 83 ●●●●

●●●

Kirk S. stands and walks over to you, a sour look on his face. He exhales sharply, snottily.

"I guess this means you won the Mow Bowl, so you can keep on mowing the grass here at the country club. Or not. Whatever." You hold out your hand for him to shake, hoping that there are no hard feelings, but he just looks at it and curls his lip in disgust. What. A. Jerk.

As you stand there with your hand held out awkwardly, the roar that you heard earlier, the one that sounds like a strange—and massive—animal, echoes in the distance. The unearthly call certainly affects the Kirks—Kirk E. and Kirk C. steer their lawn mowers away from you and Kirk S. without hesitation.

"Wait! My lawn mower is broken! I need a ride—you can't leave me here!" Kirk S. shouts at them, but they either can't hear him or don't care, because neither of them looks back or even slows down.

The noise gets louder as the ground begins to shake. Something strange is going on here. Kirk S. runs up to you, panicked.

"You have to help me. It's coming. It's not my fault! It was just too easy to use that super weed killer to keep the greens nice. How could I have known that it would get into the food chain and make . . . HIM?!"

Him? you ask yourself. Your question is answered a moment later when the sound and the rumbling reach a crescendo, and then a huge THING claws its way from underground mere feet away from you, showering you and Kirk S. with dirt, worms, and other debris—it's a mutated gopher the size of an elephant, and it looks MEAN.

"Murray," whimpers Kirk S., terrified. He jumps on the Grass Yacht. "Hurry! You have to mow us out of here!"

Murray roars when he sees Kirk S. and then dives back underground. A raised furrow of earth shoots toward you, and your next task is clear: Flee! Flee from Murray the Mutant Gopher!

You have no time to consider how this odd creature got its name. You only have time to get the heck out of here!

You whip the Grass Yacht around and hit the gas, shooting over the lip of the hill like a snowmobile in an action movie, landing so roughly on the green that it almost knocks off Kirk S. He manages to hang on, though, and you aim the riding mower back across the green, toward safety. But it's not going to be easy, because you can see from the line of disturbed earth that's on your trail that Murray is following you. Go, go, go! Or, rather, mow, mow, mow!

You're driving the Grass Yacht across the greens of Lawndon Acres Country Club in a mad dash to get to safety as Murray, the giant mutant gopher, chases you and your passenger. Ahead of you, you can see the Shed in the distance, but beside you to your right, you can see the line that Murray's making in the earth as he digs underground. Suddenly the line turns ninety degrees and heads directly toward you, aiming for your side. What do you do?

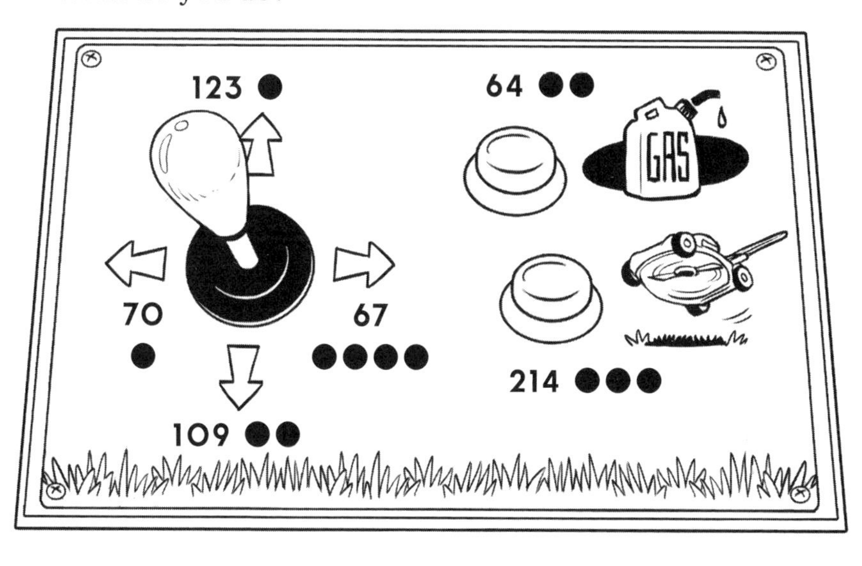

●●●●

The ground beneath your feet falls away, and you both begin to plummet to your shared doom below. Your gazes meet, and you bump fists together, making one last Fantastic Fist. The force of the explosion can't save you, but it feels RAD.

YOU ARE DEAD. CONTINUE: Y/N?

Y: Head to 101 ●●●● N: Head to 248 ●●

●

You steer to the left, and Kirk S. passes by you harmlessly. Turning the Grass Yacht around, you once again face off from opposite ends of the Mow Bowl. You each rev your engines, then accelerate toward each other again! Pick another move.

Head back to 225 ●

●●

You advance on the gathered R.A.T. horde, and they cower before you. Maybe you should, like, hit them? With things like fists, feet or, if you have it, maybe a crowbar? Hmm . . . move again!

Head back to 243 ●●●●

Standing on the far side of the now-bridgeless gap, you and your partner allow each other a wry smile and then turn to face the path ahead: From here it's a straight shot to the R.A.T. headquarters, a fact underscored by the giant floating sign above your heads that flashes the word "GO!" along with an arrow pointing in the direction of the smoking volcano lair. Giving each other a thumbs-up, you run ahead into danger . . .

A huge gate is cut into the living rock of the volcano, large enough to allow all kinds of things access to its interior . . . It's the perfect place for an evil organization bent on world domination to call home. Together, you pass through the cavernous opening, into a hangar filled with deadly dirigibles, fighter jets, and hovercraft tanks, and plenty of uniformed cannon fodder. But strangely enough, none of them attack. They all either studiously ignore you while working or studiously ignore you while not working. It's like you're not even there. At the far end of the hangar there's another, smaller but still large door, above which is a flashing neon sign that reads "GO!" Figuring that a flashing sign in a video game pointing you in a direction wouldn't point you in the

WRONG direction, you both proceed.

Soon, after a quick trek through the tunnels of the R.A.T. hole, you emerge into what must be the center of the volcano. Looking above you, you can see the sky through the opening at the top; glancing around, you spot computer workstations lining the walls on multiple levels, their monitors displaying various evil plans and diabolical charts, and dot matrix printers spitting out sinister spreadsheets. If you weren't sure before, this would confirm you were in a lair of some sort. And if you were still skeptical, the sight directly ahead of you would confirm it 100 percent, for sitting on a throne set upon a dais at the top of some steps carved from obsidian, in the middle of a large circular platform surrounded by lava, is the leader of R.A.T.: KING RAT! He's flanked by a dishonor guard of low-level R.A.T.s, and hanging from the ceiling are banners emblazoned with R.A.T.'s logo. Next to the throne is what looks like a high-tech portable toilet (wait, what?), and directly behind the throne is a mass of strange machinery that looks like some sort of battle or construction vehicle bristling with weapons. As you both glare at King Rat, your clothes torn from your travails but your resolve never stronger, he cackles dismissively.

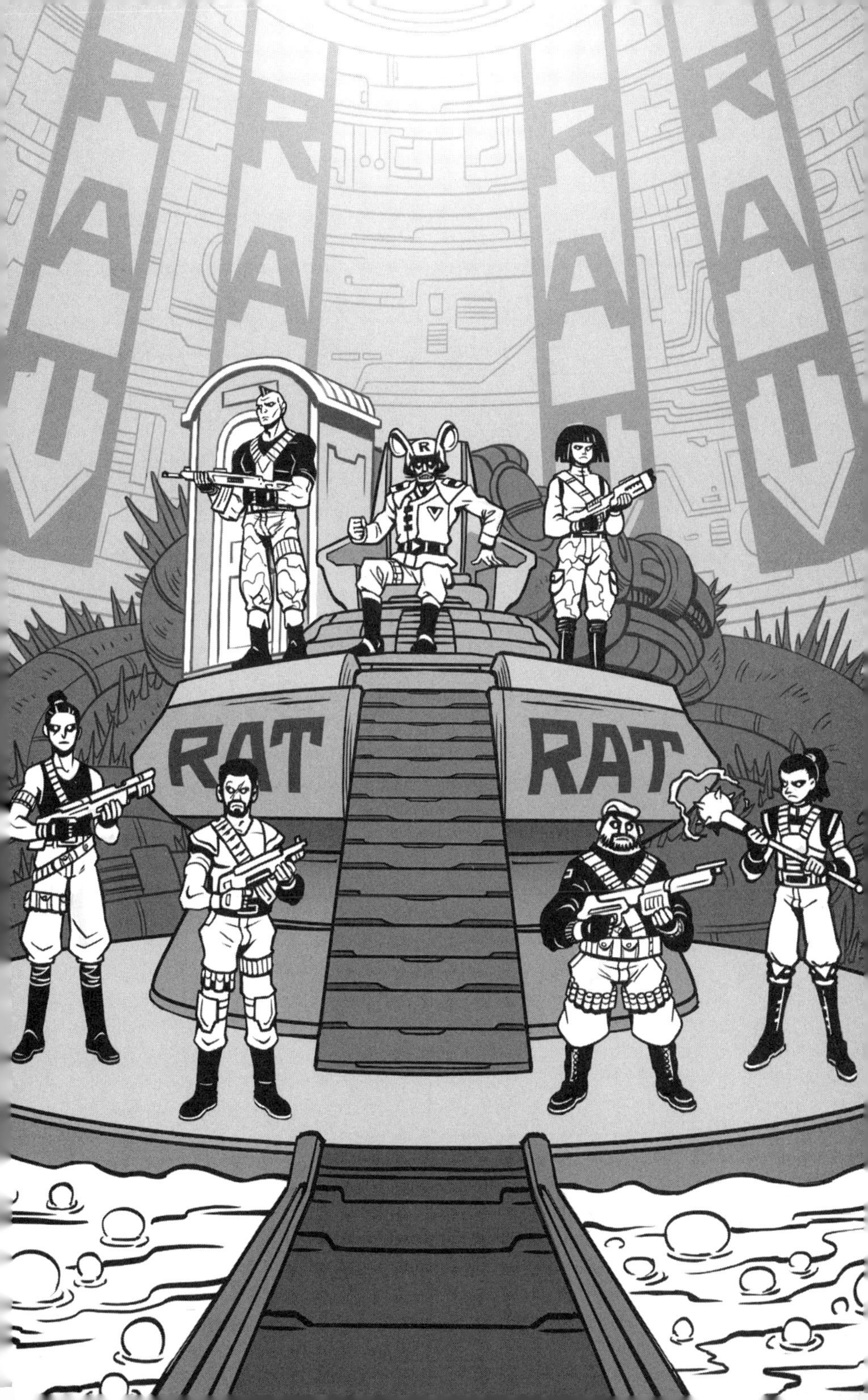
RAT
RAT

"Pathetic members of F.I.S.T.S.—I should have known that you would attempt to foil my evil plan this time, as you and your cohorts have done so many times in the past to my OTHER evil plans. That's very annoying, by the way. I would like to succeed with at least one out of every ten evil plans. Maybe we should do something like an evil plan rewards card, where every time I try an evil plan, I get a stamp or a hole punch on a card, and after nine evil plans, I turn in my card and get to execute my next evil plan with minimal to no interference. Actually, that's not such a bad idea . . ."

Realizing that he's mostly talking to himself, King Rat sits higher in his seat and fixes his attention back on the both of you. His top lip curls into an evil arch, and then he pushes a button on the arm of his throne. The portable toilet thing glows and crackles and steams, and then the door opens and two figures emerge: Pistolwhip and Dobermann Pincer! You turn to each other, disbelief on your faces—you both defeated them earlier. *What gives?* you both think.

"I bet you're thinking, 'What gives?'" King Rat says. "This is what gives—R.A.T. has developed technology that allows our operatives to blink their eyes a few times and disappear if they're defeated in combat, and they re-spawn here, in our headquarters, in this modified portable toilet (this is a prototype; don't judge), ready to fight again. Nifty, eh? We call it . . . the R.A.T. Hole!"

So THAT'S how that works in video games, you think. *That explains a lot. Huh!*

"And no longer shall we skulk in the shadows," he continues, "covertly trying to subvert and undermine and gnaw at the scraps the world leaves. Rats aren't very scary, are they? They're gross, and sometimes cute, but not terrifying. No, from now on, we are going on the attack, and to that end, R.A.T. is rebranding! From now on, you can call us . . . S.N.A.K.E.!"

The assembled R.A.T.—er, sorry, S.N.A.K.E.—minions cheer as brand-new S.N.A.K.E. banners unfurl from the rafters of the volcano, covering the old and dirty R.A.T. banners.

"And before you ask, no, we don't know what S.N.A.K.E. stands for yet. We've kidnapped top copywriters from around the world to figure that out in multiple languages, and we have some promising ideas up on the board. And when we solve that problem, the world will quake . . . quake before S.N.A.K.E.!"

The minions cheer again. It's a very easy crowd.

"But before we can wrap the world in our viselike

grip, one last thing must be accomplished—crushing the might of F.I.S.T.S.! And what better way to do it than to disrupt the wedding of its two best operatives and lure them here to their doom, eh? Eh?"

King Rat presses a button on the arm of his throne, and his chair rises from its place, hovering on a jet of energy. Then, it moves over to the machinery behind him and settles into the head of it, fitting in perfectly. You realize now that your intuition was correct. The throne really is sitting at the head of a machine body now. The battle vehicle comes to life and begins to thrash around menacingly.

"And as R.A.T. evolves, so do I! I am no longer King Rat—from now on, call me King Snake, and cower before the might of my King Snake Crawler! Attack, Pistolwhip and Dobermann Pincer! But save some for me!"

This is it. There's no denying it—this is the final boss battle of *Fantastic Fist*. Without a doubt, this is going to be your toughest battle yet. But as you two look at each other, you know there's no battle you wouldn't gladly fight as long as you're together.

Are you ready?

Well, then: Fight!

Pistolwhip and Dobermann Pincer stand before you, and behind them is King Snake in his King Snake Crawler. You won't be able to defeat him until you take out his two lieutenants, so what do you do?

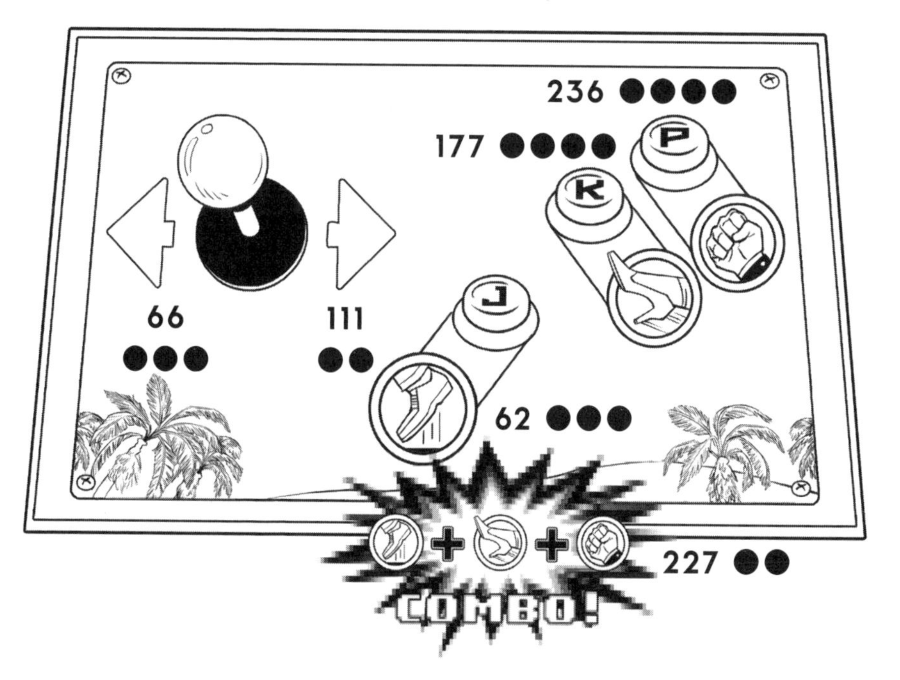

You've out-gophered Murray again, and you're almost at the Shed. You can see Rodney the golfer, the other Kirks, the Mechanic, and a crowd of snooty country club members cheering you on. You can make it! You know you can. And then Murray bursts from the ground in front of you, blocking your way. He roars his mutant gopher roar, and you can smell his mutant gopher breath. This is it—your next move is life or death. Don't choke!

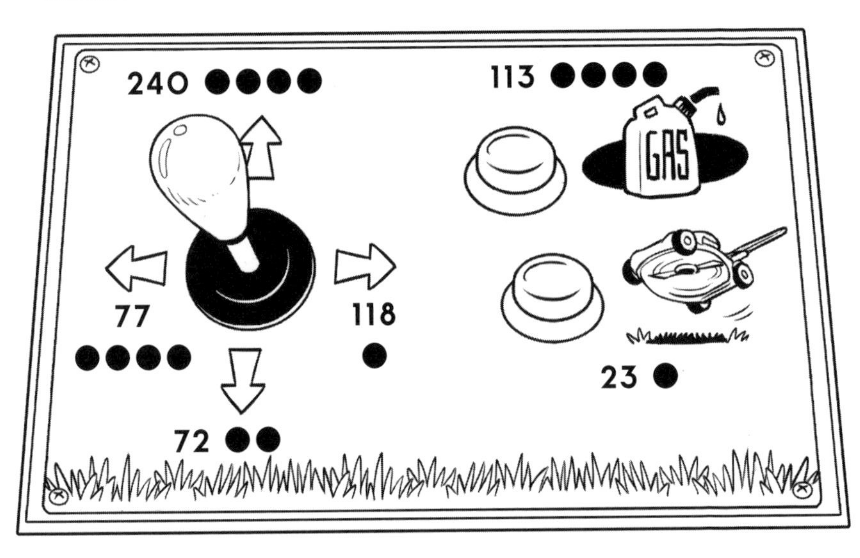

●

You unfortunately cannot dodge a blast from a laser pistol by walking backward away from it. Physics doesn't work that way, and neither do lasers. In fact, they work by being MUCH faster than you, and Pistolwhip is a good shot. That means . . .

YOU ARE DEAD. CONTINUE: Y/N?

Y: Head to 229 ●●● N: Head to 248 ●●

●●

You keep pushing forward, ignoring the stop sign. That's too bad, because as you enter the intersection, a car coming from the left zooms through the crossroads, smashing into the Mow-Luxe and reducing it to spare parts, leaving you holding the now-detached handlebar. The Hedgelordz catch up to you, smiling evilly.

"You were warned, kid," says Cutter as he and the other two Hedgelordz approach. "Now it's time for you to learn a lesson!" As they get closer, you understand that . . .

YOUR LAWNMOWER IS DEAD (AND SO ARE YOU). CONTINUE: Y/N?

Y: Head to 207 ●●● N: Head to 248 ●●

●●●

A R.A.T. creeps up on you, and you drop low to the ground, sweeping your leg at his in a dance-floor-appropriate break-dance-esque move. It works! But then another one wants to dance, and another one. You can keep kicking all day, but it seems like they'll keep coming. You need to do something else.

Head back to 243 ●●●●

You hit the gas and zoom the Grass Yacht straight toward Kirk S., and you and he are on a collision course in a lawn-care version of chicken!

Head to 125 ●●

●

You decide to fly directly into the path of the oncoming rocket of death, and if you ever wanted to meet a missile up close and personal, now's your chance because it's coming through the cockpit windshield right . . .

. . . NOW!

YOU ARE DEAD. CONTINUE: Y/N?

Y: Head to 222 ●●●● N: Head to 248 ●●

MowTown Level 3 VineLand

"You've got something special, kid," says the Mechanic, who's at the wheel of the Grass Yacht. He's driving his beloved machine away from Lawndon Acres, up a narrow lane that leads even farther up the hill. You're riding behind him, and you can see the entirety of Lawndon spread out below you, its green spaces looking neat and tidy and well-manicured. You've come a long way since this morning, and you're wondering what sort of horticultural challenges could lie ahead, and how they could possibly compare to lawn-care street gangs or giant gophers mutated by weed killer. The Mechanic must be able to read your mind, or at least be able to read moods in the same way he can diagnose engine problems from the sound of a motor, because he responds to your unspoken question.

"No one in MowTown really knows much about Vineland, except that it's got some really beautiful gardens and hedge mazes that have grown totally wild over the years. The owner is supposed to be some plant-obsessed dude who brought back some peculiar vine from an overseas trip. They planted it, and that thing took over the whole place. Kudzu ain't got nothin' on it. Some folks even say it's a magic vine. Intelligent. How do you like that, huh? Every lawn ranger in town's been dying to have a crack at it. You think you can get it under control?"

The Grass Yacht pulls up to an ornate iron gate in the middle of a tall stone wall. Both the gate and the wall are covered in vines, and although you know your eyes must be playing tricks on you, it looks like the vines are slowly MOVING. Weird.

You gulp as you jump from your perch on the Grass Yacht. You didn't bring the Mow-Luxe along, as the Mechanic told you that they'd have the tools you'd need for the job at Vineland. *That's great*, you think, but as you approach the gate, you feel . . . unarmed. Vulnerable without your trusty mower, unprotected once separated from your vehicle. But knowing how games work and getting used to the weird ways of *MowTown*, you figure that soon you'll be wielding . . . some sort of gardening implement. You just have to find it.

You pull at the gate, tearing some vines as you create a gap big enough to slip through. Once you're in, you turn back to the Mechanic. He gives you a thumbs-up, which you return, and then pivots the Grass Yacht around and heads back down the hill. You are alone in Vineland.

From where you stand, you can see that a path extends before you through an overgrown and wild garden, up the hill, and to a stone mansion that once was mighty and proud but now appears neglected. The vines of Vineland are creeping up its walls and pulling at its bricks and mortar. Besides the verdant plant life around you and the click and buzz of summer insects, there are no other signs of life . . . human life, at least. So: What do you do?

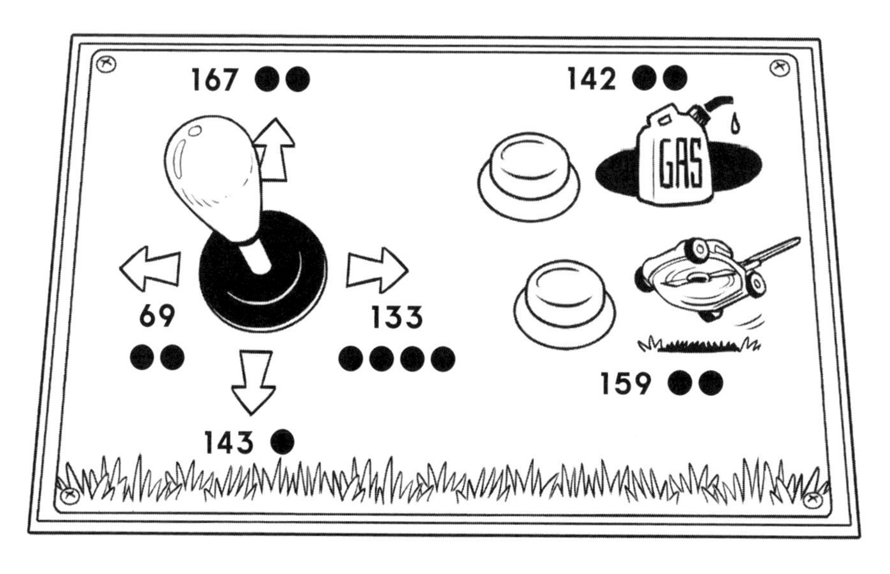

●●●

You both kick at the top of the King Snake Crawler, and King Snake responds reflexively by slamming on the brakes, sending you both flying off the vehicle. Seeing that he has you in his sights, the villain puts his wicked wagon back into gear and heads straight toward you. It's too late!

YOU ARE DEAD. CONTINUE: Y/N?

Y: Head to 216 ●●●● N: Head to 248 ●●

Figuring that research can't hurt, you decide to look around your bedroom and see if there are any clues around to help you with your mission.

At first glance, your room seems pretty ordinary; it's messy, just like your bedroom in the real world, with clothes strewn about and old plates and cups stacked in strange and inconvenient places. But it's when you look closer that you begin noticing the little differences. Your bookshelves are lined with tomes about the history of lawn care, novels about a duo of siblings called the Clipper twins who apparently solve horticultural mysteries, and well-worn manuals of various models of lawn mowers. Above your desk, there's even a calendar with a different lawn-care implement featured every month. Wherever you are—and you have to remind yourself that you're in the video game world of Lawndon, aka "MowTown"—they REALLY like cutting the grass.

From outside your window, you hear the sound of voices raised in boisterous discussion and some laughing. There's an edge to the sounds, as if the people speaking aren't the nicest folks in the world. But it's a sign of life. Hmm . . .

Do you look out the window to see what's going on? If so, head to 78 ●

If you want to keep looking around the room, head to 181 ●●●

●

You can't stand the sound of King Snake whining. It's especially annoying that he's all talk and seemingly no action. As he chatters on and on, you realize that this is what evil masterminds do in movies, distract the hero with their incessant talking. And you will not be distracted!

You move forward off King Snake Crawler . . . and fall directly into the lava pit beyond. That's just not good gameplaying, we're sorry.

YOU ARE DEAD. CONTINUE: Y/N?

Y: Head to 237 ● N: Head to 248 ●●

●●

You hop up and down, which does nothing to help you avoid the clutches of the topiary creatures, which descend upon you from both sides and wrap you in their viny, brawny, thorny arms. Sad to say, but . . .

YOU ARE DEAD. CONTINUE: Y/N?

Y: Head to 129 ● N: Head to 248 ●●

●●●

Pistolwhip charges you in a fury, and you wait . . . and then kick, your foot snaking out toward her face and sending her flying backward! She lands on the ground, unconscious. Raise that eyebrow and raise it high. You deserve it.

Head to 222 ●●●●

●●●●

You advance directly toward the monster's mouth . . . and run right down its throat. But we've got to hand it to you: If you're going to go, that's a spectacularly fantastic way to do it. Slow clap, kid. Slow, slow clap.

YOU ARE DEAD. CONTINUE: Y/N?

Y: Head to 170 ●● N: Head to 248 ●●

●

You pull back on the helicopter's controls, but that only slows it down. The missile, therefore, reaches you a second before it would have normally, blowing up the helicopter a second earlier, saving some time for the missile at least.

YOU ARE DEAD. CONTINUE: Y/N?

Y: Head to 94 ●●●● N: Head to 248 ●●

The area you've found yourself in is a small garden dedicated to topiary creations—bushes and hedges shaped into objects by crafty growing techniques and fastidious clipping. The topiaries here look strange, as if they were intentionally crafted to look like fearsome and weird beasts. They're scary and intimidating. And in the center of the topiary garden there sits a jagged rock, in which are embedded what look to be . . . GOLDEN HEDGE CLIPPERS? It's like they're the Excalibur of lawn care or something.

But as you contemplate the strangeness of your surroundings, you realize that you aren't actually alone. The topiary creatures are not quite as stationary as you previously thought. In fact, they've begun to move toward you from your left and your right, in a very unfriendly, quite menacing manner. They have bad intentions and they're almost upon you, so think fast, kid!

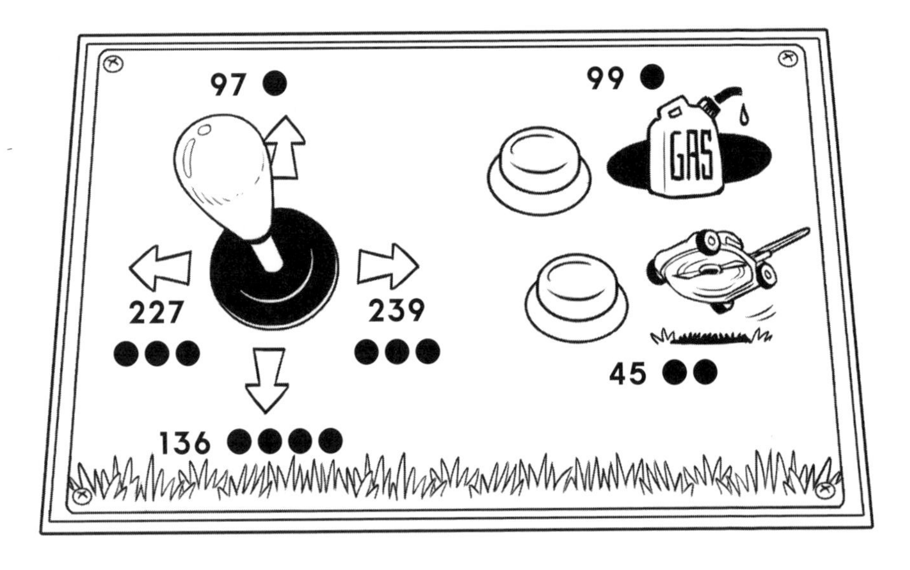

●●●

Your chopper is spinning out of control and diving directly toward the beach below! It's all you can do to make it back to the rear of the vehicle, hoping to time your next move just right . . . and right before impact, you jump, falling to the sand roughly but going directly into a twist you learned by watching all the cats that hang around the F.I.S.T.S. battle compound fall off balconies.

BOOM! The chopper explodes upon impact, its gas tanks turning it into a fireball, a fireball that engulfs you as well! You recoil from the heat, which is extreme, but . . . it's not harming you, at least in the way it should. Realizing that you're not truly in danger, you relax and walk out of the flames. Looking down at your body, you understand with a shock why the flames didn't hurt you; some of your "skin" has burned off, and you see that you are actually some sort of secret cyborg!

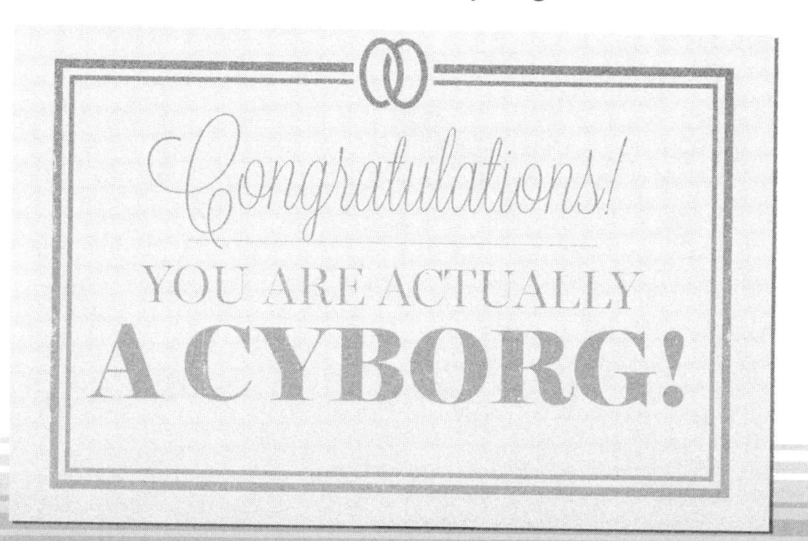

You didn't see THAT coming. Did you know this? Did the character you're inhabiting know this? Did her fiancé know?! So many questions to be answered.

Shaking your head, you walk up the beach away from the shoreline, carefully skirting around the wreckage of the chopper. Ahead of you, in the middle of a thick, impenetrable jungle, looms an extinct volcano that nevertheless puffs clouds of dark smoke—it's the lair of R.A.T., their evil base of operations where they hatch their nefarious and ill-conceived plots for world domination. Whoever ordered the disruption of your wedding is probably in there, and you want to have a word with them.

Suddenly the sand ahead of you begins to shift, as if something large hiding beneath its surface is revealing itself, and it is! It's a mustachioed man wearing a hulking exo-suit that makes him look like a strange sort of crab on two legs, complete with arms that end in two deadly-looking claws!

"Welcome to R.A.T. Island, cyborg member of F.I.S.T.S.!" he says with a slight German accent. "I have been charged by our illustrious leader to meet, greet, and then DEFEAT you in battle. Once I have vanquished you, I will take you before him, where you can learn the extent of today's nefarious and perhaps ill-conceived plot. I am the shadowy international mercenary Karl-Roberto von Dobermann or, as you may know me from my code name . . . DOBERMANN PINCER!" He snaps his serrated cybernetic crab claws to accent his name. "Now, if you please: Fight with me!"

You're on the beach. Behind you is the flaming wreck of the helicopter used to kidnap you. Ahead of you is Dobermann Pincer, an operative of R.A.T. who wants to take you to his leader, dead or alive. What's your move?

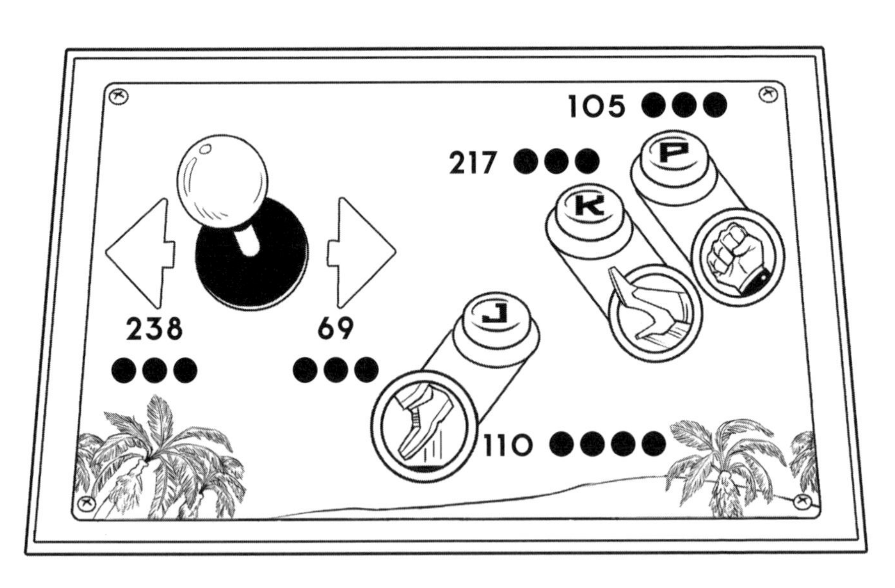

The once-mighty giant is now immobile. You approach the static mound, grab hold of some of its stray branches, and begin to pull yourself up, eventually reaching the top. From your perch, you see the Ancient Gardener walk out of Vineland and toward you. Eventually he joins you on top of the corpse of the giant copse. Looking out on Lawndon, you see the lights begin to twinkle on and hear kids getting called home for dinner. You've beaten *MowTown*, and it's time to go back to the Midnight Arcade. You feel something happening; your body begins to dissolve into an electrical mist, and as you disappear, you think to ask the Ancient Gardener a last question: "Is EVERY day like this in Lawndon?" He shrugs.

"Forget it, kid," says the Ancient Gardener. "It's MOWTOWN."

If you want to play *Fantastic Fist*, head to 185 ●●●●

If you've beaten both games, head to 248 ●●

●

There's only one Flying R.A.T. left, and this one seems to have an agenda—you can see him pressing a complex series of buttons on his small control panel, and if you aren't mistaken, you recognize that he's setting up a self-destruct doomsday protocol. Better get him before he gets you!

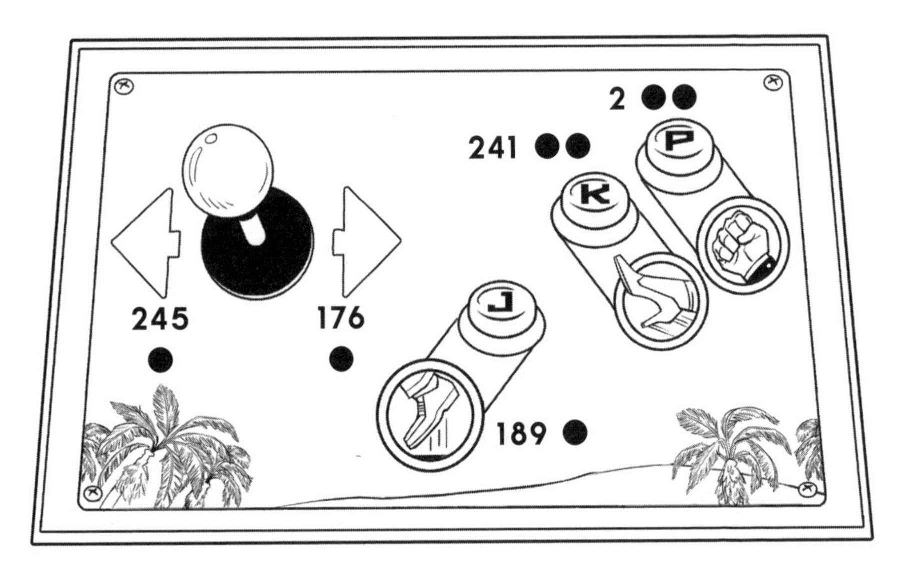

●●

You're running up your street in Lawndon at the helm of the Mow-Luxe, the Hedgelordz close behind on their Scooter Mowers. You know you've got to get to your first job before they can grab you, so you'd better choose your path wisely. Ahead, there's an intersection . . . and a stop sign! What do you do?

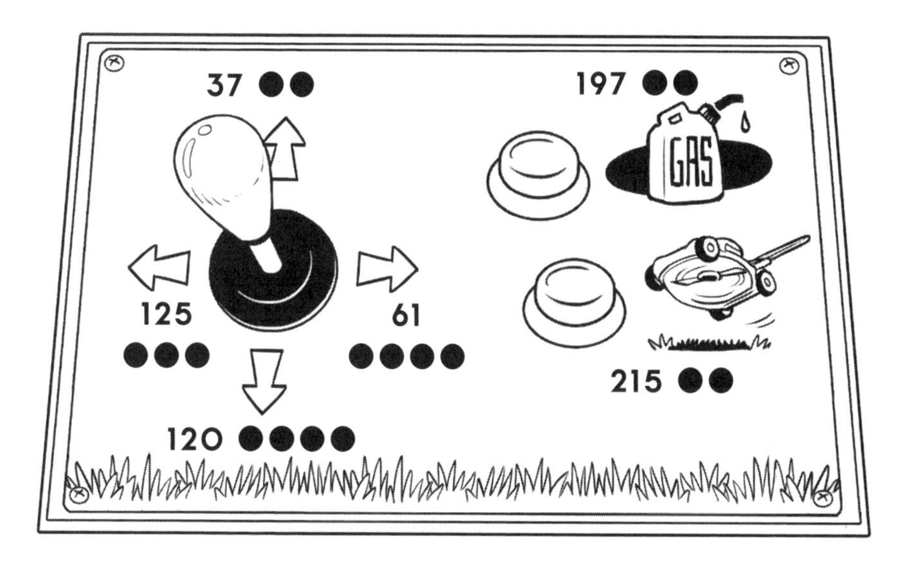

"Noooooooo! You cannot defeat me!" screams King Snake. This guy's a real whiner. "Not like this! With a press of a button, I will repair the King Snake Crawler and re-spawn my lieutenants, and we'll defeat you!" He raises his hand, ready to press the button on his control pad that will allow him to regenerate Pistolwhip and Dobermann Pincer. He's about to do it, so you'd better UNMAKE HIM!

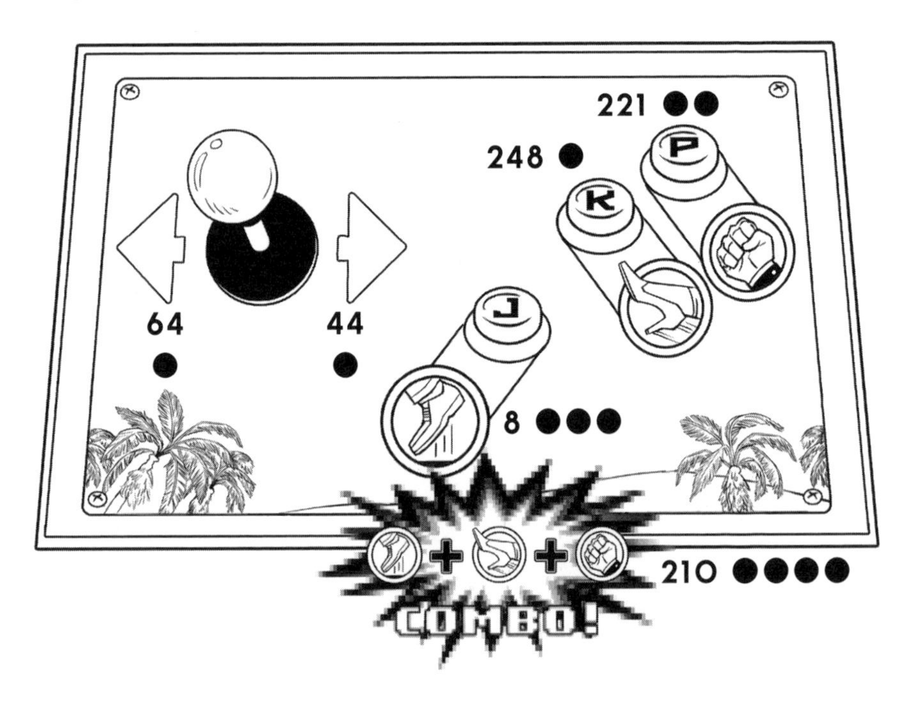

You can't slow down now! The Hedgelordz are right behind you, and you have to decide which way you're going to go. Choose again . . . but hurry. They're gaining on you!

Head back to 103 ●●●●

●

You squeeze the trigger on the right side of the helicopter's controls, sending lasers of your own into the buzzing cloud of Flying R.A.T.s, picking a few of them off. But still they come, like a terrible swarm of evil bees. Choose another move!

Head back to 222 ●●●●

You juke to the left, hoping to give the topiary creatures the runaround, but even though they don't have real eyes, they aren't fooled and move to block your way. You're trapped in the garden. Try again!

Head back to 144 ●●

You know that you can't take this lying down, even though you're currently, well, lying down. You need to get back to your wedding, and whatever plot R.A.T. is hatching, you're going to foil it . . . with your fist! You clench your cybernetic glove, concentrating and focusing your strength, and . . . success! The strong metal bindings holding your wrists together break apart, freeing you to destroy the other bindings at your feet. Thus unencumbered, you stand up in the chopper, the wind from the open door on the side whipping your hair about your head. Sensing something amiss, the copilot turns in his seat and bugs his eyes out once he sees you're free. Quickly unhooking himself from his seat belt, he taps the pilot on her shoulder, points at you, and then jumps up into a fighting stance. The pilot presses a button on her control panel, and music fills the cabin, a pulsing synth-and-drum tune that immediately gets you pumped. She hits another button, and a flashing sign lights up above you. It reads: "Ready? Fight!"

You're ready, so fight! You and the R.A.T. copilot square off, both of you primed to scrap. Then, he charges. Move it or lose it!

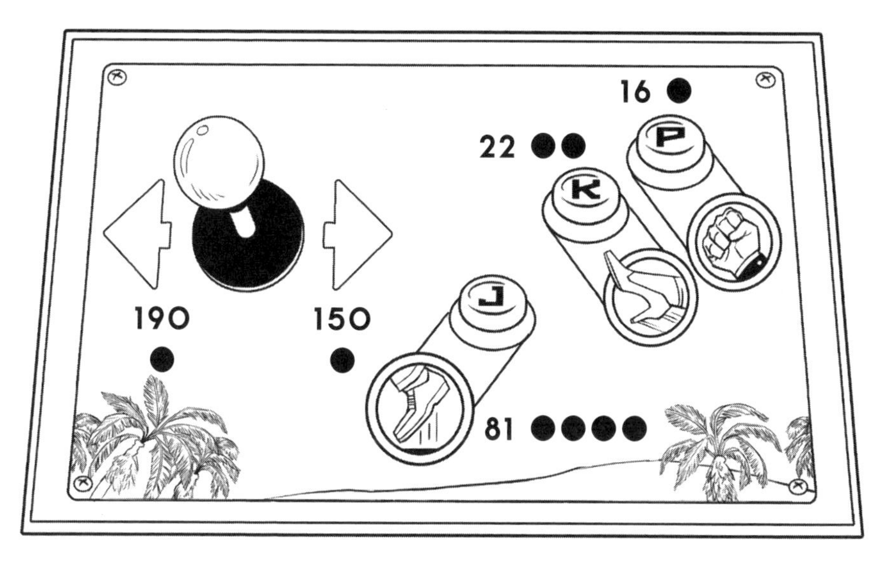

●●●●

As you approach the intersection, you squeeze the throttle again, and for a moment the Mow-Luxe trembles with power, but then it sputters and dies!

Apparently, you've flooded the engine! Rolling to a stop, you place your foot on the machine and furiously pull the cord a few times in the hopes of turning it over, but it's not working. You're still trying when Cutter and the other Hedgelordz member catch up to you and begin circling you like sharks ready to feed, if sharks rode Scooter Mowers and were part of roving lawn-care gangs. At any rate, it's . . .

GAME OVER. CONTINUE: Y/N?

Y: Head to 55 ●● N: Head to 248 ●●

●

Pistolwhip cracks her whip at you, but you dodge backward, avoiding its electric sting. Move again!

Head back to 229 ●●●

●●

Ah! Don't forget—using weapons that aren't a rake during the Mow Bowl isn't allowed! Choose another tactic before it's too late.

Head back to 125 ●●

You spring over Dobermann Pincer's head, and this delay inadvertently gives him time to recover from your last blow. The fight's starting again, so turn back to the beginning of the melee!

Head back to 49 ●●●

●●●●

You veer right at the intersection and end up pushing the Mow-Luxe directly into the path of a car! You instinctually leap to the side, but, sadly, the Mow-Luxe's instincts aren't as sharp as yours, and the vintage machine ends up getting crunched under the wheels of the vehicle. Well, it looks like your game of *MowTown* is over before it ever really began because . . .

YOUR LAWNMOWER IS DEAD.

CONTINUE: Y/N?

Y: Head to 207 ●●● N: Head to 248 ●●

●

You move to the right, and whatever's digging down there mirrors your move. You move some more, and it does the same. Panicking, you begin to run, pushing the Mow-Luxe toward what seems like an inevitable collision, and then *BAM!* The ground shoots up as if a mine exploded underground.

But that was no mine. Nope.

It was Murray.

And Murray is . . . well, let's just say that . . .

YOU ARE DEAD. CONTINUE: Y/N?

Y: Head to 10 ●● N: Head to 248 ●●

●●

You retreat, pulling the Mow-Luxe with you, but you back directly into Ms. Olsen's fence. You try to open the gate, but it's locked tight, and the snake slithers toward you. Choose again!

Head back to 160 ●●●●

You both leap into the air, hoping to deliver a devastating aerial attack, but your timing is off, allowing Pistolwhip and Dobermann Pincer to move in with simultaneous whip, pistol, and claw attacks, the might of which takes you down! You're dazed and confused, and you can hear King Snake in the background, gloating and laughing with his minions. And as you lie there on the floor of King Snake's throne room, you both reach out toward the other, hoping to touch the other's fingers before it's . . .

GAME OVER. CONTINUE: Y/N?

Y: Head to 153 ●●● N: Head to 248 ●●

●●●●

You zip through the intersection, followed closely by Cutter, who extends his rake just far enough to get it between your ankles, causing you to lose control of the Mow-Luxe, which zooms on down the road without you. It swerves into one of the trees that line the street, exploding in a fireball that lights up the tree like a torch.

You and Cutter stare at the column of flame in awe, then he turns to you and says, "I didn't do it." He peels off as a group of very angry adults begins to surround you. Metaphorically . . .

YOU ARE DEAD. CONTINUE: Y/N?

Y: Head to 103 ●●●● N: Head to 248 ●●

●

You move back to the rear of the King Snake Crawler, giving King Snake enough time to press the button! The R.A.T. Hole buzzes, and out pop Pistolwhip and Dobermann Pincer. They're back! And not only that, the King Snake Crawler seems to be automatically repairing itself somehow, the motion of which knocks you clear off the vehicle.

Head back to 216 ●●●●

●●

You hit the button on the dashboard and fire sprays from the front of the Grass Yacht, bathing you in wonderful warmth. Cool. But then Murray rams into the Grass Yacht from the side, sending you flying. Uncool.

YOU ARE DEAD. CONTINUE: Y/N?

Y: Head to 125 ●● N: Head to 248 ●●

You retreat from the King Snake Crawler's charge and find yourself at the edge of the platform surrounded by lava. You don't want to go any farther, so you'd better try something else.

Head back to 74 ●

You veer away from the brick at the last moment, and while your blades miss coming into contact with the obstacle, the wheels of the Mow-Luxe use it as an improvised ramp, sending the machine—and you—flying. And as you improbably clear Old Lady Olsen's fence and come crashing down in her neighbor's backyard, you realize that video game physics are nothing to laugh at. With that, it's . . .

GAME OVER. CONTINUE: Y/N?

Y: Head to 92 ● N: Head to 248 ●●

●

You squeeze the trigger on the left side of the controls, and a missile shoots out from beneath your chopper, exploding in the midst of the Flying R.A.T.s and sending way more than a few of them falling toward the ocean below. Might be overkill, but hey—whatever works!

Head to 203 ●●

Topiasaurus Rex gets closer and closer and closer, and just as it's almost upon you, you jump up into the air and grab on to its leg! It wasn't expecting that at all! Good strategy, kid.

Head to 110 ●●●

You and your partner move back, and Pistolwhip mocks you. "What, you two can't fight for yourselves? C'mon, let's do this!" She and Dobermann Pincer creep closer, whip, pistol, and claws at the ready. Choose again!

Head back to 29 ●●●

●●●●

You decide to turn the Grass Yacht to the right and meet Murray head-on, a contest of strength between classic lawn-care machinery and mutant brawn. But just as the lawn mower is about to collide with the line of earth disturbed by Murray's digging, Murray decides to emerge from underground, mutant mouth open wide. Kirk S. screams. You scream. And, in addition to screaming . . .

YOU ARE DEAD. CONTINUE: Y/N?

Y: Head to 125 ●● N: Head to 248 ●●

●

You turn the Mow-Luxe to the left, but it's not running, and that means it's not cutting grass! You get tangled in the long grass immediately, and while you're trying to pull free, the snake takes the opportunity to sink its fangs into your ankle. The bad news? The pain is terrible. The good news? It only lasts a moment, and then . . .

YOU ARE DEAD. CONTINUE: Y/N?

Y: Head to 95 ● N: Head to 248 ●●

●●

Your hands want to mow something, cut something, prune something, but the time isn't right. Soon, though. Soon. You can feel it. Until that time, choose again.

Head back to 235 ●

Frustrated, you punch the control panel of the helicopter with your cybernetic fist, which turns it into electronics salad. The controls are no longer responsive, so you wouldn't be able to pilot your way out of this even if you tried.

YOU ARE DEAD. CONTINUE: Y/N?

Y: Head to 94 ●●●● N: Head to 248 ●●

You rev the engine of the Mow-Luxe, but instead of it giving you a burst of speed, black smoke begins to pour from its guts. Something's wrong inside and needs to be fixed, but it's still running . . . for now. Take advantage of this time and choose another move!

Head back to 95 ●

●

You keep moving forward, but you just . . . can't . . . make it! The bridge falls from beneath your feet, and both of you follow the boulder down into the liquid tumult below. You tried, but . . .

YOU ARE DEAD. CONTINUE: Y/N?

Y: Head to 101 ●●●● N: Head to 248 ●●

●●

There's nothing in this direction but solid hedge that you can't move through.

Head back to 39 ●●

●●●

You stalk toward Dobermann Pincer, and he snaps his claws at you, grabbing your wrists firmly in them. "I see," he says, "you have no fight left within you. Very well, I shall crush you!" The claws close tighter, tighter, and then . . . *snap*.

YOU ARE DEAD. CONTINUE: Y/N?

Y: Head to 206 ●● N: Head to 248 ●●

●●●●

You hit the switch that makes the Mow-Luxe jump, and both you and the machine hop up a few inches. The Hedgelordz look at you quizzically. "What are you doing, kid? Goofing off?" Cutter says. "Well, two can play at that game."

One of the Hedgelordz leans in and whispers in his ear.

"Oh, right. There's four of us here. Whatever!" Cutter pushes you aside roughly, and he and his gang descend upon the Mow-Luxe, kicking it and smacking it with their rakes. Within minutes . . .

YOUR LAWNMOWER IS DEAD.

CONTINUE: Y/N?

Y: Head to 8 ●●●● N: Head to 248 ●●

●

You steer away from Murray's pursuit, but your evasive maneuver hasn't worked—the giant mutant gopher is still on your tail! It's gaining! The ground beneath the Grass Yacht opens up, and you, Kirk S., and the Grass Yacht all fall into a tunnel beneath the country club, where there are no lawns to mow. It's . . .

GAME OVER. CONTINUE: Y/N?

Y: Head to 125 ●● N: Head to 248 ●●

●●

You make a hard right turn into the overgrown grass, just as the snake makes to strike. It misses you, passing harmlessly over your shoulder and into the tall grass. You've managed to avoid it . . . for now! And until you meet again, you can get busy mowing. Yeahhhhhhhh!

Head to 204 ●●●

As the world falls down around you, you kick. And kick again! You're alive and kicking! (For the next few moments, until you hit the water and meet the Cyberanhas again, that is.)

YOU ARE DEAD. CONTINUE: Y/N?

Y: Head to 101 ●●●● N: Head to 248 ●●

You turn the Grass Yacht's wheel to the left, but nothing happens. "Gotta at least give it some gas first," says the Mechanic. Pick another move.

Head back to 201 ●

●

You charge at the King Snake Crawler, and the strange vehicle charges at you . . . and runs right over you both! Ow. No, that's not how that was supposed to go. Not at all. Sadly, it's . . .

GAME OVER. CONTINUE: Y/N?

Y: Head to 29 ●●● N: Head to 248 ●●

●●

You put the Grass Yacht into emergency reverse, terrified of facing the wrath of Murray, but as you back up in a panic, you drive directly onto a patch of earth weakened by his digging. The Grass Yacht tumbles down into the new sinkhole, sending you and Kirk S. flying. You both land roughly, and while you're stunned . . . well, let's just say you're easy pickings for a giant mutant gopher and leave it at that.

YOU ARE DEAD. CONTINUE: Y/N?

Y: Head to 115 ●●●● N: Head to 248 ●●

●●●

You bear down on Kirk S., not conceding an inch to the left or the right, and both of you extend your rakes toward each other, prepared to joust! You're getting closer . . . closer . . . closer . . . just hold steady . . . *CRASH!* Your rakes tangle together in a mess of metal! You let go of your rake, and in the confusion, Kirk S. loses control of his lawn mower, and the machine wobbles back and forth wildly before tipping over on its side just as he jumps clear.

Head to 24 ●●●

Kneeling, you pull the cord on the lawn mower. Once. Nothing happens. Twice. Still nothing. You try a third time, and . . . YES! The lawn mower's engine turns over, and the machine begins to shake as its inner workings come to life. It hums and chugs, and now you feel ready. You grab the handlebar again and know that when you think of using this button, you'll give the mower some extra power. Sweet.

You push the mower forward and leave the garage.

Head to 207 ●●●

•

King Snake scowls at you both and manipulates a control mechanism that makes the King Snake Crawler rise up. "So, you think that because you've defeated those has-beens that you can best me? Ha ha ha ha ha! Face the might of the King Snake Crawler!" The machine roars into action, heading straight for you—move or be moved!

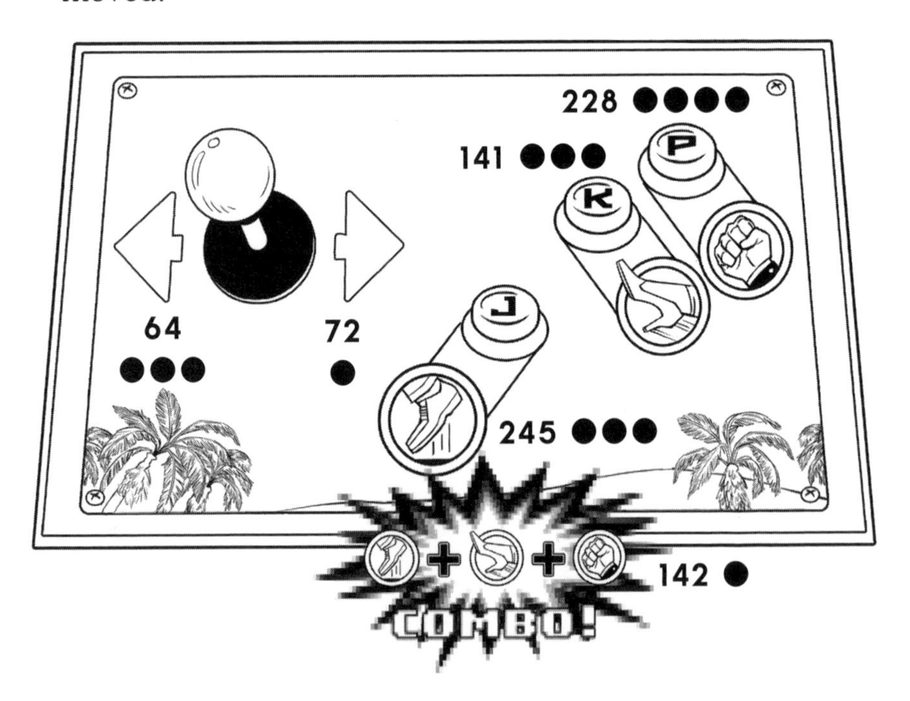

Defeated and still on fire, Murray growls loudly one last time and then sinks below the ground in retreat. You follow his progress as he digs his way back toward the far reaches of Lawndon Acres. The assembled crowd cheers, despite the grounds of the country club looking like . . . well, like a giant mutant gopher was chasing a souped-up riding lawn mower all over them. Rodney, the golfer in the loud clothes, runs over to you, golf club in one hand and a frosty glass of lemonade in the other.

"Kid! You did it! You put the kibosh on Murray! You're a lawn-care genius!" he says as he lifts you off the ground in an awkward and messy bear hug given what he's holding in his hands. Putting you down, he turns to Kirk S., who has his arms open for another hug. Rodney shakes his head. "As for you: Your buddies, the other Kirks, told me that Murray is all your fault. You're going to be spending the rest of the summer getting this golf course back into shape. Yeesh!"

Kirk S. slumps away toward his friends, dejected, as Rodney puts an arm over your shoulder.

"You've got a future here in MowTown, kid. I can spot talent when I see it," he says, taking a long sip from his lemonade. "In fact, I'm gonna help you out and put in a good word for you for another job. The ultimate job here in town. You know what I'm talking about?"

Looking longingly at the lemonade, you say that you have no idea what he's talking about.

"Are you kidding me?" Rodney says, disbelief in his eyes. "I'm gonna give you a letter of recommendation to do the yard work up there."

Rodney points into the distance, and you can see farther up the slope from town a vine-covered mansion, surrounded by massive hedges.

"Kid, I'm sending you up to Vineland," he says, forebodingly, confirming your suspicion.

Head to 39 ●●

●●●

You jump off the landing skid, but there's nothing to jump TO, and gravity takes its inevitable and, in this case, very sad course.

YOU ARE DEAD. CONTINUE: Y/N?

Y: Head to 58 ●●● N: Head to 248 ●●

●●●●

As Murray attacks, you steer hard to port, and he's left chomping empty air. Good job! But you've steered so hard, you come full circle and are facing him again. Choose another move!

Head back to 36 ●●●●

•

You poke your head outside the window to see what you can see, and your first impression is that you're in a nice green suburb. But before you can get even the beginnings of a second impression, multiple hands GRAB YOU and pull you bodily out the window! You can't see who your assailants are, but they're not being particularly gentle with you, that's for sure. Without warning, they're shoving you inside something, a big, dark bag of some kind, a bag that smells strongly of old, wet grass clippings. Gross. You cry out, asking whoever's out there to set you free, but all you get in response is a swift kick to the bag.

"Hey, shut up in there," whines one voice.

"Yeah, pipe down," says another. "You thought you were gonna try and compete with us? The Hedgelordz? Think again, lawn jockey!"

"Ha ha! That's a good one," says a third voice. "We're gonna have to teach you a lesson. What do you say, Hedgelordz?"

All three of the people outside the bag yell their approval, and you're jostled around some more as the bag you're in gets attached to something. Then, you hear the sound of a motor starting, and everything around

you begins to vibrate. What is going on?

Seemingly in answer to your question, one of the voices outside the bag speaks, this time louder, over the roar of the engine.

"Hey, kid—if you like grass so much, why don't you have a mouthful!"

You start moving, and that's when you realize that you're not in just any old bag, you're inside a LAWN MOWER BAG, you're attached to a LAWN MOWER, and, as the bag starts to fill with grass, you're MOWING A LAWN.

Outside the bag, the voices begin a call-and-response chant:

"Who mows MowTown?"

"The Hedgelordz mow MowTown!"

They repeat it over and over as the grass fills the bag—and your mouth—and you realize that it's already . . .

GAME OVER. CONTINUE: Y/N?

Y: Head to 192 ●●●● N: Head to 248 ●●

●●

You try to retreat outside, but you back into more R.A.T. minions, who quickly dog-pile—er, rat-pile—on you. Try as you might, you can't break free. You struggle, but it's . . .

GAME OVER. CONTINUE: Y/N?

Y: Head to 146 ● N: Head to 248 ●●

●●●

You try to cross the street with your mower, but the assembled Hedgelordz block your way. "Where do you think you're going, kid?" Cutter says with a sneer. "Your garage is over there. We're not going to give you another warning." Pick another move!

Head back to 207 ●●●

There's no room to jump inside the helicopter. Very low ceiling and all. Try again.

Head back to 58 ●●●

●

You back the Mow-Luxe farther into the garage and promptly crash into a refrigerator, which pops open. A shelf of sodas collapses, sending a bunch of cans to the floor, fizzing. Try something else.

Head back to 8 ●●●●

You smack an advancing R.A.T. henchman with your cybernetic fist, and he goes down, only to be replaced by another one. You repeat the action again, and again, and again. The repetition feels like a glitch in the system, and suddenly you're thrust backward in the game, forced to try a new path.

Head back to 18 ●●

You move the Mow-Luxe a little to the right to outfox the snake. Or is it outsnake the snake? Either way, the snake won't be outfoxed or outsnaked. It stares at you with hungry eyes, determined to bite you. Move again.

Head back to 89 ●●

You've knocked Dobermann Pincer onto his back, and he lies there in the sand, flailing about, helpless . . . but probably only for a moment. You can end this now if you make the right choice, so make it!

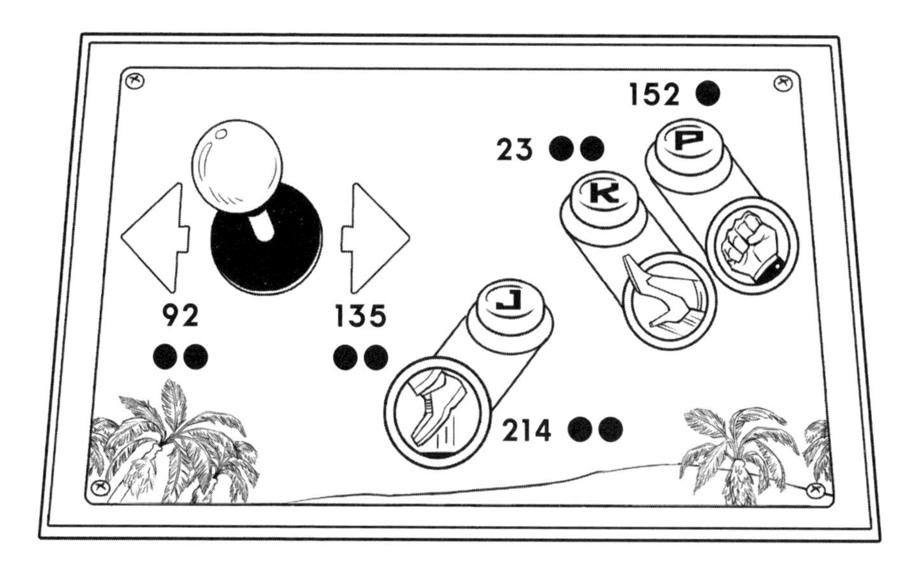

You can't believe it, but it's true—you're standing mere feet away from your sweetheart, and who is standing right in front of you. Your wedding ceremony was interrupted by a violent attack from R.A.T., but here you are, together, on the beach, bathed in the romantic light of the flaming wreckage of a helicopter. Music swells, and you both turn to look at the chopper that just landed: Captain Lu, in the pilot's seat, has turned on the vehicle's public address system, and a chip-tune version of a wedding march plays. He grins and gives you two a thumbs-up. You walk toward each other, both of you holding up your cybernetic fists. Once you're close, you both bring your arms back . . . and fist-bump, your amazing cybernetic gauntlets coming together with an impact that sends out a shock wave. Energy crackles around you, the strength of your union filling you with power.

"Fantastic Fist!" booms Captain Lu's voice over the PA (and you recognize it—it's the voice in the game's attract mode back in the Midnight Arcade!) as the music switches to another chip-tune, a speedy, action-movie version of Mendelssohn's "Wedding March." You feel married . . . and pumped for some action! "And congratulations!" Captain Lu adds as he lifts off in the chopper—wait, why is he leaving?—and the music somehow stays behind. If anything, that's a cue, and you both turn around to take in the island—the volcano lair of R.A.T. lies before you, and you know that you have to make it there and take them down. You walk up the beach, and as you come to the crest of a sand dune, you can see ahead of you a jungle that you must traverse to get to the volcano.

You look at each other, wink, and side-scroll into the jungle . . . together.

Cautiously you proceed into the jungle, your eyes ever on the volcano in the distance but knowing that at any moment the defenses of R.A.T. could manifest themselves in some fashion—and there MUST be something here defending the perimeter of their headquarters. But for now, there's nothing, and you take these moments of relative calm to reassess your gameplay—you're no longer one person, you're two people, and you're going to be fighting together. You don't feel like much has changed, actually. If anything, you feel MORE complete, like a team. You do know that your control scheme has changed slightly, though, and that you have a new special attack at your disposal: the Fantastic Fist Bump, the move that you performed back on the beach. You also know that you can't use it too much and have to save it for when you really need it. Cool.

Within moments, you come to a rope bridge that reaches across a raging river that cuts through the jungle. You step on it cautiously, and the moment your feet touch its surface, the sound of alarms begins echoing through the trees, the horns drowning out the sounds of the tropical birds.

The waters below you begin to roil even more, and strange large fish break the surface in leaps of uncanny height, arcing directly over the path in front of you.

They're cybernetic piranhas—Cyberanhas!—terrible R.A.T. creations built to chomp whoever tries to cross the bridge! You both back up, but there's a sound from behind you—rolling down the path you just came down is a huge boulder, and it's headed straight toward you!

What do you do, newlyweds? There's a boulder behind you and a treacherous rope bridge beset by Cyberanhas ahead. Make a move, and hurry!

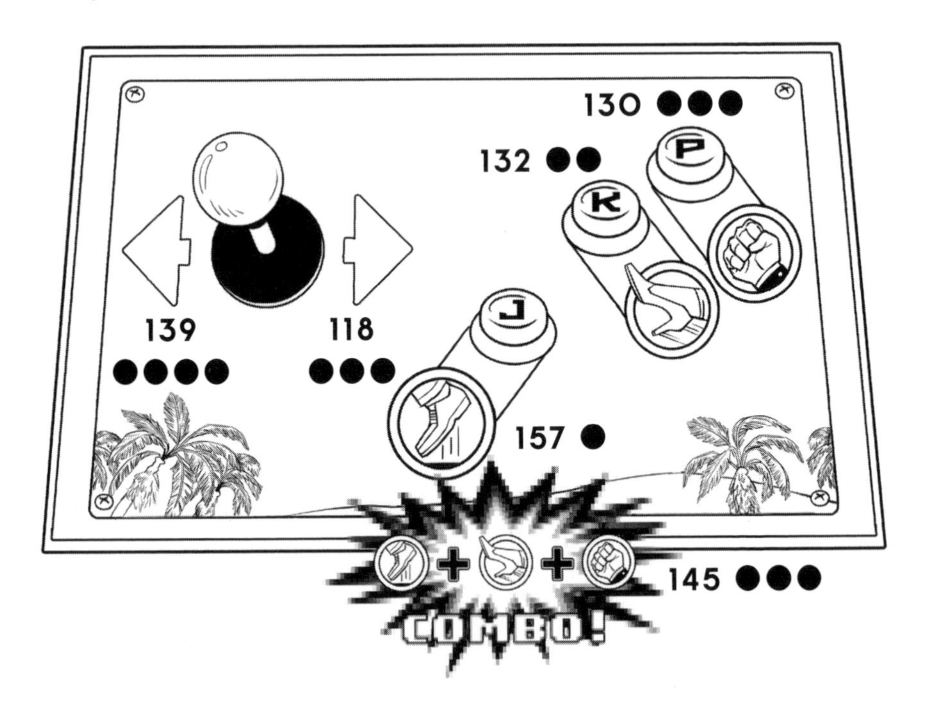

●●

You've taken a few circuits around Old Lady Olsen's yard, and what was once an impenetrable riot of greenery has become a typical suburban backyard. Reaching the edge of the property, you turn the Mow-Luxe around and notice that you're not quite done. There remains in the middle of the yard one last tall tuft. Yes, you missed a spot, and you push the Mow-Luxe in its direction, figuring that you'll finish with a flourish.

And that's when the snake returns, slithering out of its hiding place. From its movements, you can see that it intends to defend its grassy home, but you can't let that happen—you've got a job to do for Old Lady Olsen. The fate of the yard is at stake. What's your move?

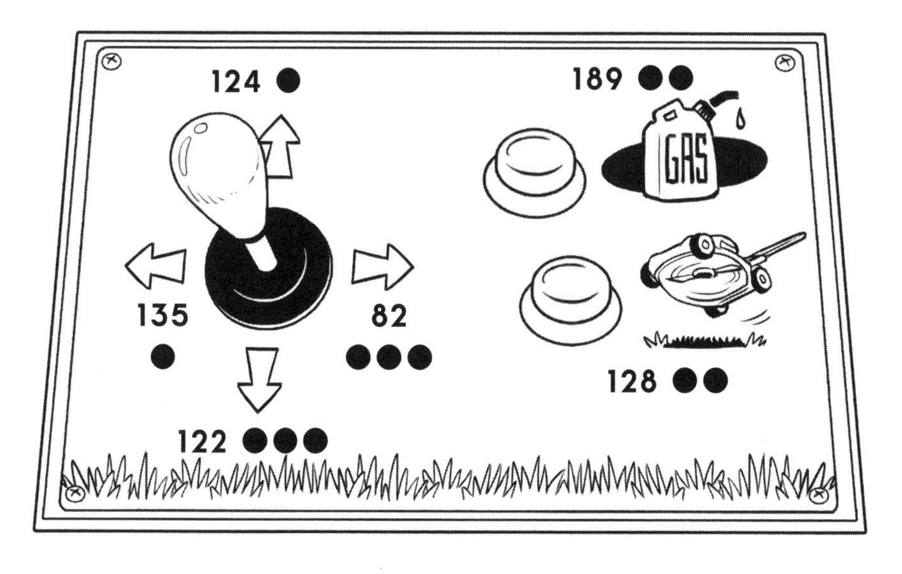

You aim a kick at Pistolwhip, hoping to take her out with one swift karate move, but her whip finds your leg as it extends, hugging your ankle tight. You fall to the ground, and when you're prone and helpless, Pistolwhip laughs nastily and gives you a dose of juice, the electricity moving up your leg and throughout your body instantaneously. This would have made a great story to tell your kids about your wedding, if only you had survived.

YOU ARE DEAD. CONTINUE: Y/N?

Y: Head to 243 ●●●● N: Head to 248 ●●

You jump into the air, and one of the R.A.T. thugs catches you, holding you by your waist as you extend your arms out to the side. A ballad begins to play over the sound system—you glance at the DJ booth and see that the DJ is there, spinning tracks. He points at you and winks—this was supposed to be the song for your first dance! And then you notice that your dance partner is still holding you aloft and is running toward the glass wall that overlooks the water . . . and he throws you through it with a crash! As you fall toward the rocks below, you can't help but think that this really was a wedding to remember.

YOU ARE DEAD. CONTINUE: Y/N?

Y: Head to 18 ●● N: Head to 248 ●●

●

Your Mow-Luxe is purring, and the snake is coiling up for an attack. It's now or never, so make a move!

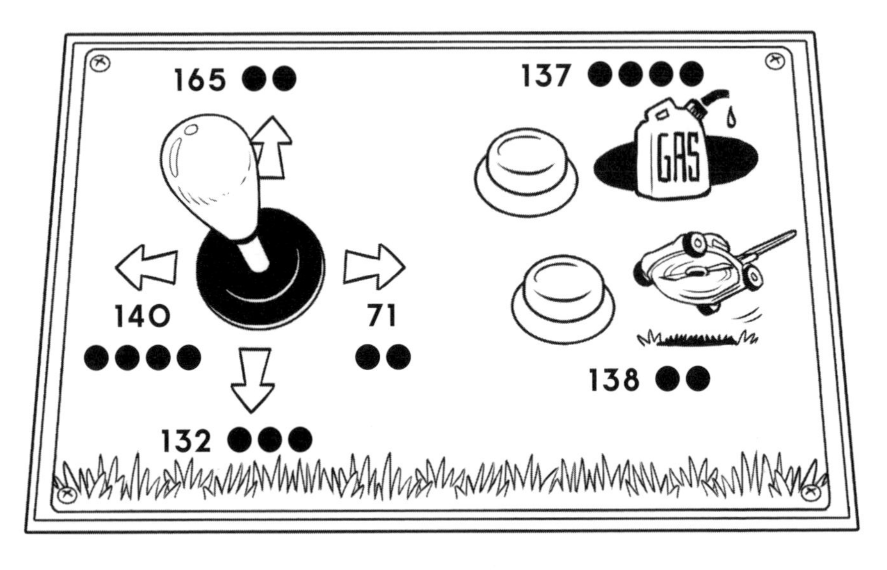

●●

No! No! You didn't seize the moment, and now you see Dobermann Pincer flip backward into a fighting stance. "Come to me," he sneers. "You are no match for my fighting prowess, obviously," he says, not without a hint of condescension. You gave him too much time, and now you have to begin the fight again.

Head back to 49 ●●●

●●●

You go toward the edge of the garden, and as you come to the wall, the previously sluggish vines come to active life, whipping out with ferocious speed and, in an instant, wrapping around you tightly. However hard you try, you can't break free, and you are pulled inexorably into the hedge! You are now a part of Vineland, and . . .

YOU ARE DEAD. CONTINUE: Y/N?

Y: Head to 129 ● N: Head to 248 ●●

You fall out of the chopper but just manage to grab ahold of one of its landing skids at the last moment, grasping it with both hands. As you hang there, the R.A.T. pilot somersaults out of the door of the weaving, now-pilotless chopper and grips the landing skid as well, facing you and ready to fight. What's your play?

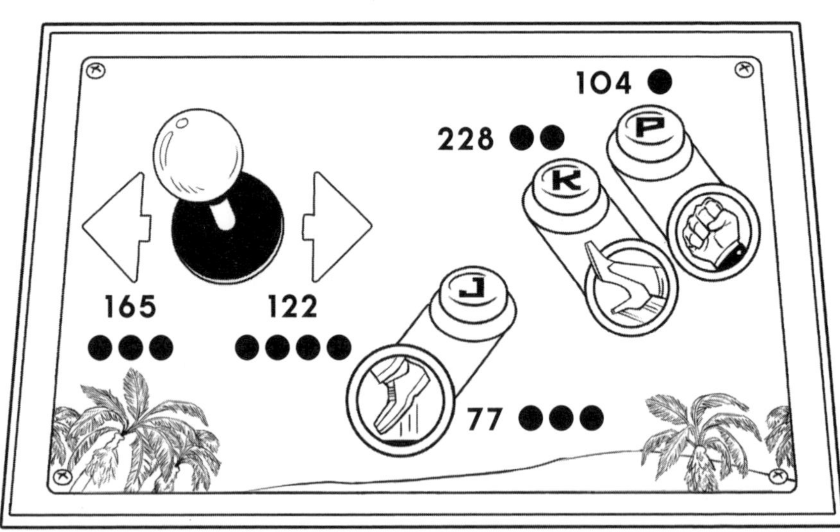

●

You've successfully made the last turn, and you're approaching another intersection. Ahead, the road continues. The street on your left ends in a cul-de-sac; on your right, a kid is walking their dog; and behind you, it's Cutter! Even though you've eliminated two of the Hedgelordz, he hasn't given up, and now he has his rake in one hand, extending it toward you in an attempt to trip you up.

Whither will thou mowest?

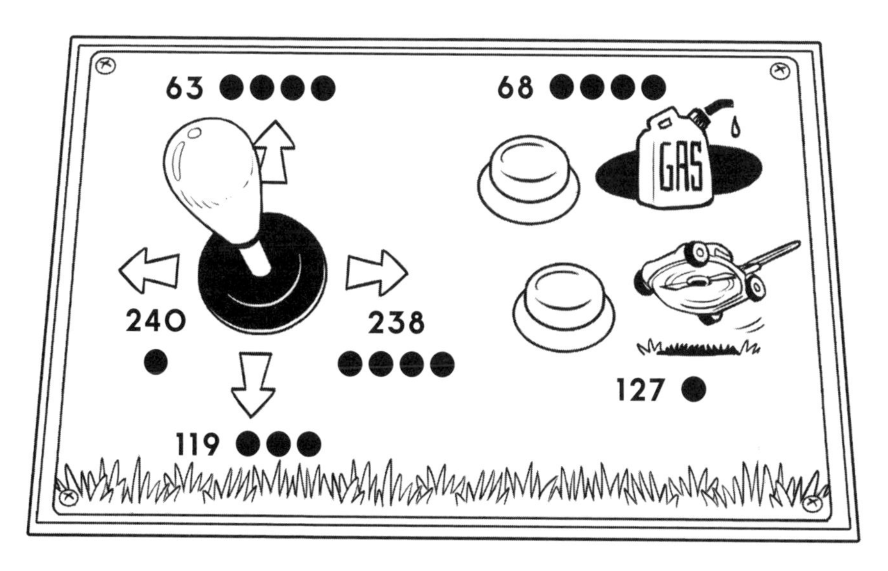

●●

You pull back on the controls, and the helicopter rears up, the missile passing harmlessly beneath you. That was close! But now the Flying R.A.T. is vulnerable. Take it home!

Head to 54 ●

You jump up and take the Mow-Luxe with you, clearing the ground by a good few inches. This must be the way you raise the lawn mower's blade and also avoid obstacles in your path. Good to know. This will come in handy later, but for now, try something else.

Head back to 8 ●●●●

You're perched atop the King Snake Crawler, in the perfect position to deal a decisive blow, but . . . you keep moving, until you fall off its backside. King Snake chortles and turns the machine around to make a go at you both, and now you go back to the last move.

Head back to 216 ●●●●

You rush forward toward the rock in the middle of the garden as the topiary creatures descend upon you, just avoiding them. They get snarled and caught together as their branches tangle, and in the confusion, you reach the rock. Feeling an irresistible urge, you clutch both handles of the clippers and pull. At first, they're stuck, seemingly fixed permanently, but you redouble your efforts, and . . . they slide out, accompanied by a fantastic chiming sound effect that comes from nowhere and everywhere.

Head to 144 ●●

●●

Punching fire SOUNDS like a good concept, sure, but in practice it's just not very effective against a fountain of fire, and by "not very" we mean "not at all." And that means . . .

YOU ARE DEAD. CONTINUE: Y/N?

Y: Head to 74 ● N: Head to 248 ●●

As Topiasaurus Rex rushes at you, you zig to the left at the last possible moment, and the monster passes harmlessly by. Roaring in frustration, it turns around and runs toward you again. Choose another move!

Head back to 3 ●

You throw a punch with your special fist just as Pistolwhip snaps her whip, and the weapon wraps itself around your hand. She snarls and activates her whip's charge, which shoots into your cybernetic hand, gets absorbed, and shoots back at her! Wincing, she drops the whip. You've disarmed her—at least partially!

Head to 3 ●●●●

●

You've encountered your fair share of overgrown gardens, but these topiary monsters are the wildest things you've ever seen. You wonder who would have grown them and what kind of fertilizer they must have used. But you've got no time to think more on it. You have decided to act.

You flail your arms at the topiary creatures, getting scratches all over your body in the process. But your wild movements hold them off for a moment, which gives you another second to choose another action!

Head back to 47 ●●

●●

Figuring that there's no way you can win any sort of battle here, with the Rakes having the home-lawn advantage, you reluctantly turn the steering wheel in the direction from whence you came, motoring up the bank of the hill of the bowl you're in. You can hear the Kirks gloating over your retreat, their haughty laughter somehow piercing through the sound of the Grass Yacht's motor. You think that perhaps you can finish your job and get out of the game some other way, but deep inside you know that not challenging those upper-class "lawn jocks" means that it's . . .

GAME OVER. CONTINUE: Y/N?

Y: Head to 201 ● N: Head to 248 ●●

You gun the Mow-Luxe's throttle, and as you do, the thing digging underneath the pleasant slopes of Lawndon Acres erupts from its subterranean lair, and you end up meeting Murray a lot sooner than you probably should have. Yes . . .

YOU ARE DEAD. CONTINUE: Y/N?

Y: Head to 10 ●● N: Head to 248 ●●

You're halfway across the bridge, and the boulder is rolling after you, closing the distance on the rickety span. The only way is forward, but another Cyberanha, a BIG one, is arcing across your path, and its jaws can't be avoided. What's your move?

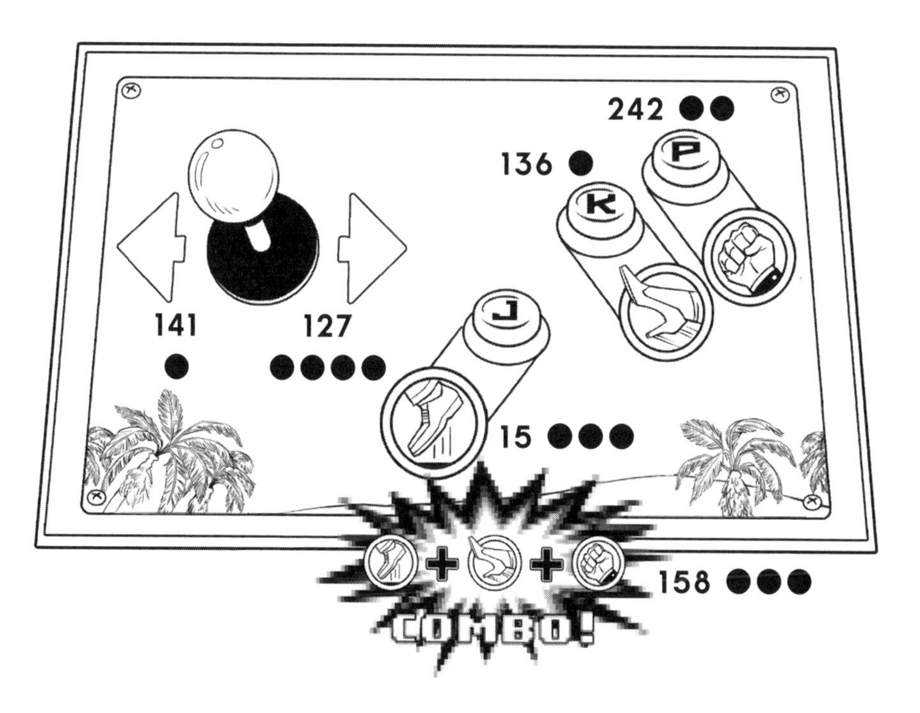

●

You try to punt away Pistolwhip's laser blast with a well-timed kick but instead leave yourself open to being roasted by its VERY hot bolt of energy. *Ouch*, you think as you slip to the ground. Love hurts!

YOU ARE DEAD. CONTINUE: Y/N?

Y: Head to 229 ●●● N: Head to 248 ●●

●●

You push the Mow-Luxe forward, but there's something lacking, something you've forgotten to do. It just feels lifeless. Attempt a different move.

Head back to 8 ●●●●

Safely on top of the King Snake Crawler, you both unleash a volley of punches on its head, ripping into its metal hide and exposing its inner workings. It looks like you are trying to destroy the metallic surfboard you're riding. The weird vehicle writhes and shudders. You've almost destroyed it!

Head to 56 ●●●

●●●●

You've gained a little distance on the Hedgelordz, but they're still coming after you! Ahead of you there's another intersection, beyond which is another stretch of road. On the corner on your right, there's a yard with an overgrown carpet of green, and to your left, there's another car, but this one's waiting patiently at a stop sign. Where do you go?

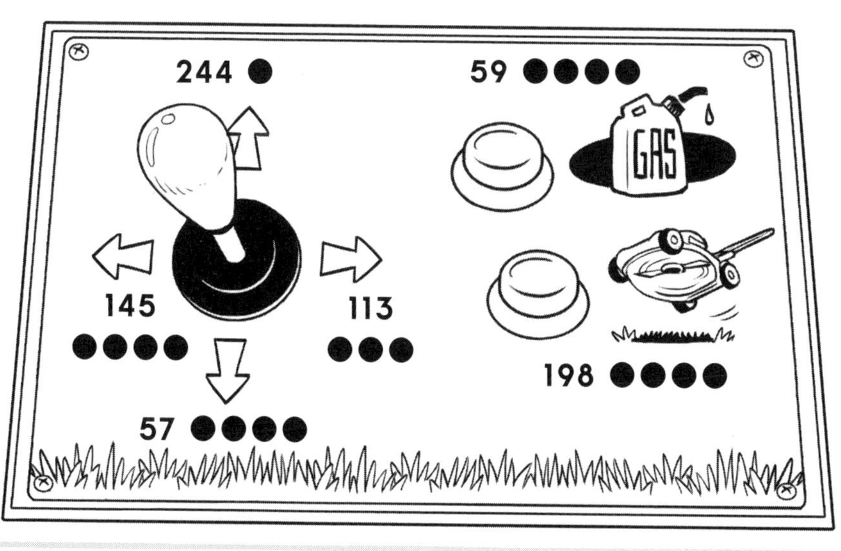

●

You take a swing at the R.A.T., connecting solidly and knocking her off the landing skid. But as you do, the chopper lurches, causing you to lose your grip with the other hand. As you and the R.A.T. fall toward the ocean, she looks at you and shrugs. *What can ya do?* her expression seems to say in the moment before you hit the water's surface. What indeed.

YOU ARE DEAD. CONTINUE: Y/N?

Y: Head to 58 ●●● N: Head to 248 ●●

●●

You back away from Topiasaurus Rex's maw of jagged wood and roots, and it snaps at where you were a second ago. Angered, it begins to attack again, so you must move again!

Head back to 178 ●

You punch Dobermann Pincer once in the chest, solidly connecting and driving him back a few feet. He looks shocked, as if he didn't expect that. Surprise him again!

Head to 169 ●

The only thing over there is a bunch of old camping equipment, which will be useful in *CampTown*, the sequel to *MowTown*. But the time for sequels is later. Now it is the time to MOW! Try again.

Head back to 8 ●●●●

You choose your character with the Select button within your soul, and as you do, you feel your essence hurtling toward the couple at the speed of light, and . . .

. . . you're inside a body! And looking down at yourself, you see that you're dressed up in a tasteful and very functional wedding dress. You're the bride!

Momentarily bewildered by your surroundings, you're not ready when the thugs from R.A.T. descend upon you, overwhelming you with their sheer numbers. You try to reach out to your sweetheart and he to you, but a crowd of cretins are threatening him and blocking his way and preventing you from reaching each other. The creeps surrounding you bind you with ultra-strong restraints. Thus captured, you are grabbed and tossed bodily into their waiting chopper, and once loaded, they lift off, leaving the wedding brawl behind.

You lie still in the back of the aircraft as it begins to glide over the open ocean, figuring that it's better to keep cool and see if you can get any valuable intelligence about R.A.T.'s attack on your wedding. Sure enough, the R.A.T. flunkies who grabbed you can't keep their flunky mouths shut.

"So, any word on why the boss wanted us to break up that F.I.S.T.S. wedding and snatch the bride?" asks the copilot.

"No idea," responds the pilot. "Some kind of nefarious plot, I'd guess. Our orders are just to take her back to the volcano lair and present her to King Rat. I'm just a pilot and a thug. Questions like that are above my pay grade."

"I hear that. I wonder what's for lunch in the commissary today."

"Veggie burgers, I think."

"Aw. I thought today was meatloaf."

"What? The veggie burgers are good, you just gotta give 'em a chance . . ."

You tune out their inane flunky chatter and think—you're restrained in a helicopter flying high above the ocean, heading toward the island hideout of R.A.T., the sworn enemies of F.I.S.T.S.—what can you do about it? Your options are limited: You COULD be calm about it and just wait and see, or you could bust out of your restraints and start a midair melee with these two goons. What do you do?

If you wait and see what happens, head to 7 ●●

If you decide to cut loose, head to 58 ●●●

●●

At your command, the Grass Yacht slows down, and Murray misses you as he crosses in front of the lawn mower, but a second later, you run into the huge furrow he's left in the ground. The impact sends you and Kirk S. flying through the air and then crashing down. Not only are the grounds of Lawndon Acres torn up, it's . . .

GAME OVER. CONTINUE: Y/N?

Y: Head to 125 ●● N: Head to 248 ●●

You've grabbed on to the leg of Topiasaurus Rex, and the creature looks like it's ready to swat you off. Knowing your giant-killing lore, you begin to scramble UP Topiasaurus Rex's leg, then torso, deftly avoiding its grasping plant claws. Up, up, up! Until you've reached its shoulder! You're standing on Topiasaurus Rex's left shoulder, next to one of its three heads. It doesn't seem to have noticed you've reached that perch yet, so . . . what move do you make?

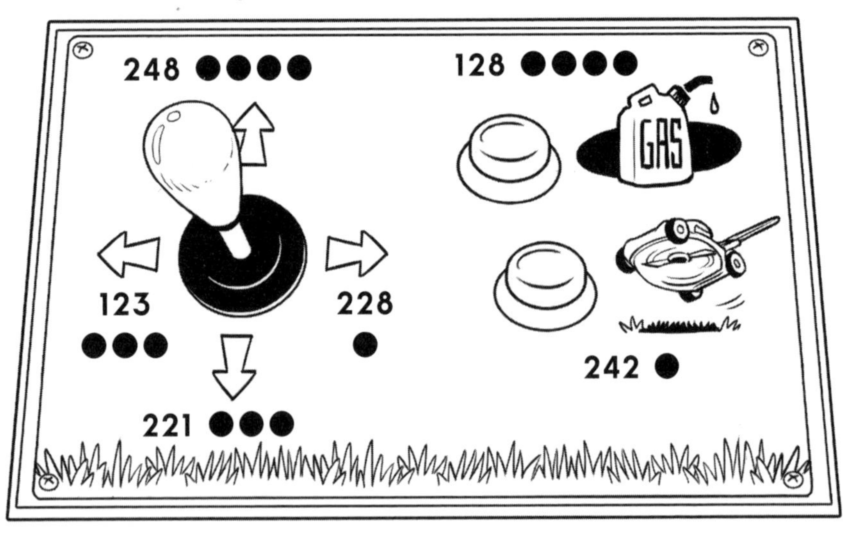

●●●●

You launch yourself into the air, and Dobermann Pincer slices at you with his claws as you move, driving you back to the ground. He wants a fight, so you'd better give it to him. Move again.

Head back to 49 ●●●

●

You go faster . . . and drive directly into the sinkhole! That was . . . a strategy, to be sure. An unworkable strategy, but a strategy all the same.

YOU ARE DEAD. CONTINUE: Y/N?

Y: Head to 24 ●●● N: Head to 248 ●●

●●

You and your partner run forward toward Dobermann Pincer and Pistolwhip, and they both brandish their weapons, ready to do battle. Pick another move!

Head back to 29 ●●●

●●●

You run toward the topiary creatures, the Golden Clippers raised over your head. They would have been more effective aimed AT the monsters. Perhaps in your next life you'll clip them. For now, though . . .

YOU ARE DEAD. CONTINUE: Y/N?

Y: Head to 47 ●● N: Head to 248 ●●

●●●●

When you squeeze the right trigger, lasers meet the missile in midair, blowing it up! You pass through the cloud of its explosion only to see that the Flying R.A.T. has launched another attack, so you'd better try again!

Head back to 203 ●●

●

You lean on the Grass Yacht's steering column and barely, just barely, manage to make it around the sinkhole. Whoa. Great mowing, kid.

Head to 36 ●●●●

Did you twitch? Because that move cost you your perch on the King Snake Crawler, and you both fall back down to the ground again, and King Snake takes immediate advantage of this and rolls right over you!

YOU ARE DEAD. CONTINUE: Y/N?

Y: Head to 216 ●●●● N: Head to 248 ●●

You turn the Mow-Luxe to the right, not even bothering to wait to get to the intersection, instead hopping the curb and cutting a neat line in the grass of the lawn on the corner. Clippings fly directly into the face of the Hedgelordz member next to Cutter, causing them to sputter and wipe out on their Scooter Mower. You've successfully made your turn, but Cutter's getting closer!

Head to 95 ●

You pound on the gas button and a stream of fire from the Grass Yacht's flamethrower envelops Murray. The giant mutant gopher howls and begins to pat the flames out, thrashing wildly and ignoring you entirely. But Murray's efforts are in vain, for the strange chemicals that mutated him have also made him incredibly flammable, and, well . . . the details are pretty gory. How about we just say: You did it! You've beaten Murray! Yay!

Head to 75 ●●

●

You didn't find the lemonade. Well, it's somewhere back in the game. Without it, you can't carry on. You're completely spent. In fact, you can barely even respond as Topiasaurus Rex's last remaining head swoops down. Carnivorous plants, right?

YOU ARE DEAD. CONTINUE: Y/N?

Y: Head to 129 ● N: Head to 248 ●●

●●

You hop up in your seat, but that's it. This move does nothing in the helicopter. Choose another move.

Head back to 222 ●●●●

●●●

You try moving left, but there's no grass to mow in the garage. C'mon. Get going (and get mowing)!

Head back to 8 ●●●●

You've successfully evaded Murray so far. Now he's on your left and has turned his course to be parallel with the Grass Yacht. He's going faster now and starts to pull ahead, like he's racing you. But then, the line left by his tunneling disappears—you can't see where he's gone! Suddenly a giant hole opens up in front of you; that crafty mutant dug a sinkhole to trap you!

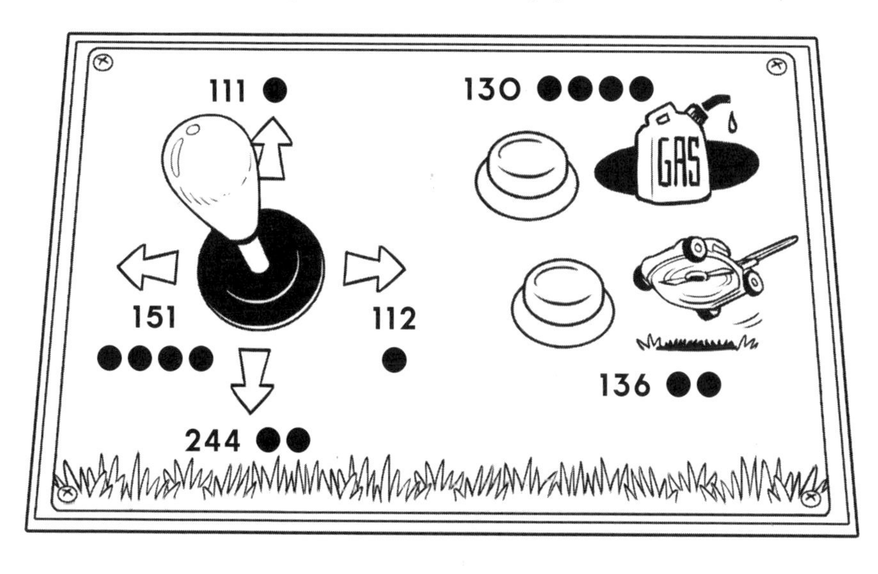

●

You accelerate toward the brick, which accomplishes only one thing: You smash into it sooner. The impact causes the Mow-Luxe to shake, then shiver, then go *KA-CHUNK-KA-CHUNK-KA-CHUNK-KA-CHUNK-SKREEEEEEEE*, and then break into tiny pieces. Your mowing time has ended . . . and that's when you hear the hissing of the snake. You forgot about the snake, didn't you? Yes, that means . . .

YOU ARE DEAD. CONTINUE: Y/N?

Y: Head to 92 ● N: Head to 248 ●●

●●

You pull the lawn mower backward, directly into the Hedgelordz. Cutter laughs. "I thought you'd chicken out," he says as he roughly shoves you aside. "Hedgelordz, let's party!" he says, and he and his flunkies descend upon your Mow-Luxe, stomping it down and reducing it to a heap of metallic junk in minutes.

YOUR LAWNMOWER IS DEAD. CONTINUE: Y/N?

Y: Head to 8 ●●●● N: Head to 248 ●●

●●●

You jump up, bringing the Mow-Luxe with you, and the sound and vibration of its impact startles the snake, saving you from its jaws, if only momentarily. You've bought yourself some time, so pick another move.

Head back to 160 ●●●●

●

You have nothing to operate here, nor are you holding anything to mow or cut with, so this does nothing. At least for now. Choose another action.

Head back to 129 ●

●●

Attempting to sneak past the topiary creatures, you try to dodge to the right and slip out of the dead end. They're too quick for you, though, and they block you from running away. Choose another action.

Head back to 144 ●●

You both run forward, ducking the chomping jaws of a Cyberanha and making it about a third of the way across the bridge. Now to make it the rest of the way.

Head to 101 ●●●●

●

Murray lunges as you turn the wheel of the Grass Yacht hard to starboard, and his claws gouge the green, but you're unharmed. Fantastic work, but you're so tensed up that you end up turning right back around to face him again. Do something else!

Head back to 36 ●●●●

●●

You meekly push your lawn mower back up your driveway and into your garage, followed by the laughter of the Hedgelordz. Once you're inside, Cutter reaches up and grabs the garage door and closes it roughly, leaving you and the Mow-Luxe in the dark. The gang's Scooter Mowers start up, and you can hear them speed away, still laughing. You wait a moment until the sound fades, then attempt to lift the door. No dice! They've locked you in! You pound on the door, yelling for help, but no one can hear you over the hum of lawn mowers in the neighborhood. Sadly, it's . . .

GAME OVER. CONTINUE: Y/N?

Y: Head to 8 ●●●● N: Head to 248 ●●

You put on the brakes, but unfortunately Cutter does not, and he and his Scooter Mower crash into you, a collision that sends both of you flying and crunches your mowers together. Dazed, you both lie in the middle of the street. Mowing season has begun, but neither of you has a mower, so it's . . .

GAME OVER. CONTINUE: Y/N?

Y: Head to 103 ●●●● N: Head to 248 ●●

●●●●

Mindful of traffic laws, you slow down for the stop sign. It's good you did, too, for a car drives through the intersection right when you would have been in the middle of it, had you kept going. Ironically, though, your attention to safety has allowed the Hedgelordz to catch up to you, and as they surround you on their Scooter Mowers, cutting off all means of escape, you realize that . . .

YOU ARE DEAD. CONTINUE: Y/N?

Y: Head to 207 ●●● N: Head to 248 ●●

●

The Grass Yacht hops up and down a couple of times, which gives Kirk S. the opportunity to drive his lawn mower directly into its side and, using his momentum, push you over, causing you to tumble to the grass!

And it's a good thing, too, if you can believe it. Sure, you are now on the grass and a little banged up, but you hear an unpleasant sound coming from the Grass Yacht and you're now weirdly thankful to be on the ground.

Something sparks in your engine, igniting your gas tank, and the Grass Yacht explodes in a fireball, complete with mushroom cloud. As you sit there staring at the conflagration in disbelief, the Kirks drive up to you on their lawn mowers.

Kirk S. couldn't look more smug if he tried. He laughs, looking down at you on the grass.

"Let that be a lesson to you," he says. "Never try to out-mow your superiors." Yes, he's a jerk, but it's still . . .

GAME OVER. CONTINUE: Y/N?

Y: Head to 154 ●●●● N: Head to 248 ●●

●●

Squeezing the left trigger on the helicopter's controls shoots a missile at the oncoming object . . . and blows it up! But their combined explosive power is too much, and the cloud of fire envelops both you and the Flying R.A.T.! At least you took him with you, right?

YOU ARE DEAD. CONTINUE: Y/N?

Y: Head to 222 ●●●● N: Head to 248 ●●

You back up, and the snake mirrors your action, retreating back into the grass, its eyes fixed upon you. Try another move.

Head back to 89 ●●

You move forward, hand over hand, and the R.A.T. retreats, sticking out her tongue at you while she does it. What is she, five? Try another move.

Head back to 94 ●●●●

●

You push the Grass Yacht forward, going fast enough that Murray passes just behind you. Phew, that was close!

Head to 115 ●●●●

●●

You rush directly into the flamethrower's spray, and that goes about as well as you'd think it would, which is to say not well at ALL.

YOU ARE DEAD. CONTINUE: Y/N?

Y: Head to 74 ● N: Head to 248 ●●

●●●

Topiasaurus Rex may be big, but its shoulder is narrow, and there isn't much room to move here, much less room for error. Moving to the left is DEFINITELY an error, and you slip from its shoulder and tumble back down below.

YOU ARE DEAD. CONTINUE: Y/N?

Y: Head to 3 ● N: Head to 248 ●●

●●●●

You throw the Grass Yacht into reverse, effectively putting on the brakes, and while you're switching gears, Kirk S. gets even closer. Before you can react and defend yourself, his rake hooks into you and pulls you out of your seat as he passes. You fall to the ground with a thud and watch your lawn mower zip off backward. You've lost the Mow Bowl challenge, and now it's . . .

GAME OVER. CONTINUE: Y/N?

Y: Head to 225 ● N: Head to 248 ●●

●

You push the Mow-Luxe toward the snake, but at the last moment it dodges to the side, allowing you to go past it, like a matador avoiding a bull. The Mow-Luxe cuts the remaining grass, but as it does, the snake whips around and bites you! You've finished the job, but the snake has finished YOU. It's . . .

GAME OVER. CONTINUE: Y/N?

Y: Head to 204 ●●● N: Head to 248 ●●

●●

You and Kirk S. are getting closer and closer, on course for a head-on lawn-mower collision. What's your move?

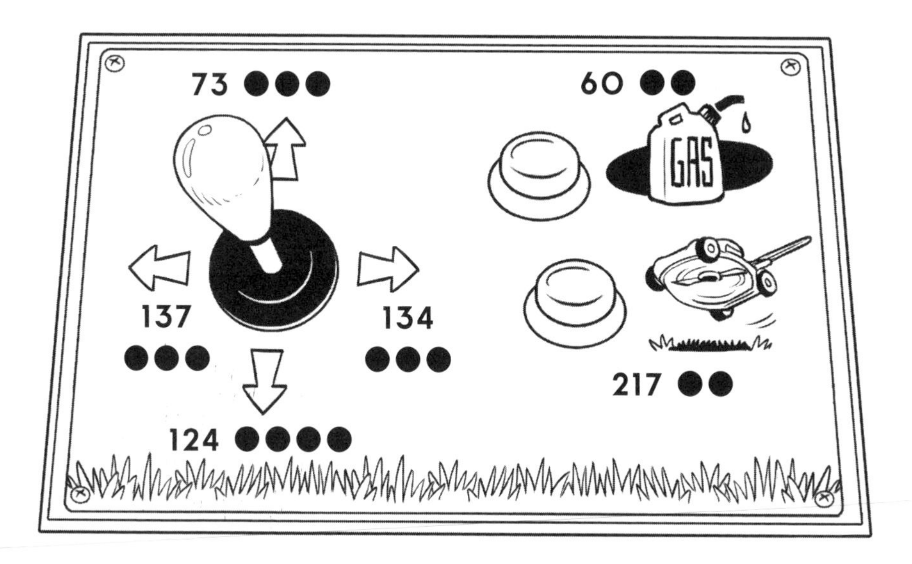

●●●

You turn left at the intersection . . . directly into the path of an oncoming car! You swerve to avoid it and end up colliding with a pile of bags containing fresh lawn clippings. The impact sends you flying, and you end up lying dazed on the lawn of one of your neighbors, admiring the skill of whoever cut the grass as the Hedgelordz loom over you.

YOU ARE DEAD. CONTINUE: Y/N?

Y: Head to 207 ●●● N: Head to 248 ●●

●●●●

You move backward, and as you do, Dobermann Pincer snaps out of his stunned state. "Aha," he says. "You are a coward, no? Afraid of me? Well, I'll give you a reason to be afraid!" Go back to the start of the fight!

Head back to 49 ●●●

●

You move to the right edge of the little garden, and as you get closer to the wall of vegetation, you see a flash of white somewhere within. Curious, you pull aside some leaves and reveal what's inside: It's a SKULL! And then you notice that the vines on the wall are moving, extending themselves toward you! You jump back to the center of the garden, out of their reach. Pick another move!

Head back to 235 ●

●●

Holding hands, you leap ABOVE the stream of flame, landing on top of the King Snake Crawler, a move that completely surprises King Snake. Well done!

Head to 237 ●

●●●

Creeped out by this strange little place, you turn around and walk back to the crossroads you just left.

Head to 129 ●

You continue to run across the bridge, directly into the gaping tooth-and-metal maw of the Cyberanha! It's not much comfort, but its mouth is actually big enough to swallow two people, so at least you and your beloved get devoured together. How sweet.

YOU ARE DEAD. CONTINUE: Y/N?

Y: Head to 84 ● N: Head to 248 ●●

●

The Mow-Luxe bounces a few inches above the road, but hey, there's nothing there to bounce OVER. Try something else.

Head back to 95 ●

●●

The Mow-Luxe hops up again, but this time there's nothing to hop over. This time you just look like a kid holding on to a hopping lawn mower, which is kind of weird. Stop hopping. Start mowing. Pick another move.

Head back to 89 ●●

You hit Dobermann Pincer with your other fist, and this blow sends him spinning, but he still won't fall. Pick another move!

Head back to 169 ●

Knowing that you should probably attack while the attacking's good, you furiously start to work on clipping the neck of the head immediately in front of you. You send debris flying in all directions, and before you know it, you've severed not one but TWO of its heads! Amazing!

Head to 170 ●●

●

You're at the crossroads in the messy, overgrown hedge maze that leads to the Vineland estate. The path ahead is clear and seems to lead straight to the steps of the mansion, but the paths to the right and left are darker, more overgrown, and mysterious.

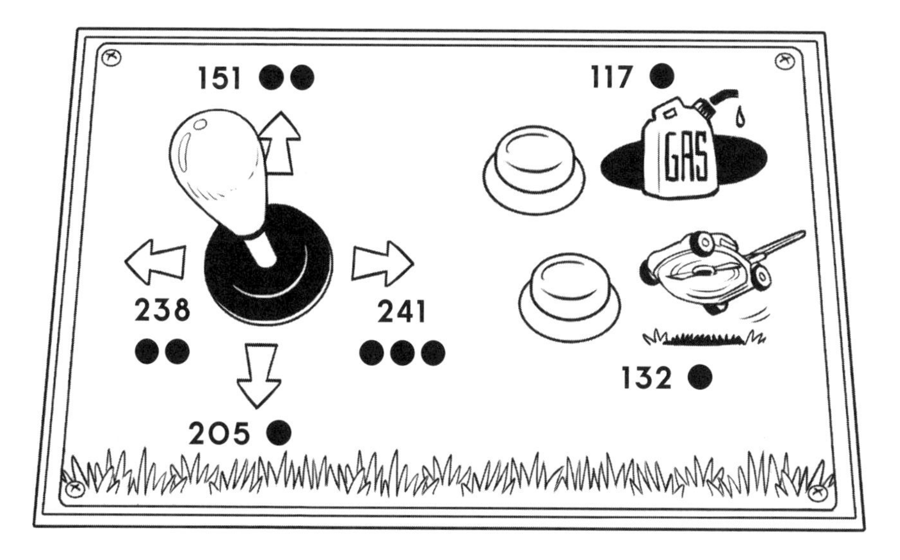

●●

You start jumping before you reach the object, thinking that it might magically come to life and start attacking you. Vineland has already proven to be a trippy place, so the idea is not that far-fetched. However, as you move, you start to forget what you were doing in the first place, and even why you're here. You notice a glitch in your vision and sense that something is happening, and then . . .

Head to 47 ●●

You punch the Cyberanhas in midair, your fists turning them into mists of fish guts and spare parts. But the boulder is getting closer, and you're no farther along the bridge. Get going and choose again!

Head back to 84 ●

You decide to send caution to the wind along with a huge spray of ignited gas. That's right. You've selected the Flamethrower option because you like living on the edge. I mean, you've got nothing to lose at this point, so why not try to ignite everything in sight?

The Grass Yacht's flamethrower sends out a bloom of fire as it falls into the sinkhole, and you figure that even though you failed, the sight of a flaming riding lawn mower falling into huge pit in the middle of a golf course probably looks cool to whoever's watching.

YOU ARE DEAD. CONTINUE: Y/N?

Y: Head to 24 ●●● N: Head to 248 ●●

●

You jump. You land. Then you choose again.

Head back to 129 ●

●●

You rapidly pick off Cyberanhas with well-placed kicks, sending them flying back to the water, but you still need to get ACROSS the bridge! Move again!

Head back to 84 ●

You retreat with the Mow-Luxe, and the snake follows you back, until you touch the border of Old Lady Olsen's fence. Seeing that you have nowhere to go, the snake rises to strike . . . choose again!

Head back to 92 ●

That way lies an impenetrable wall of vines and roots that you couldn't cut through without a pair of magical hedge clippers, which would be rad to have, but you don't. Magical hedge clippers—pshaw! Pick another move.

Head back to 39 ●●

●

Nope! The Fantastic Fist has yet to fully charge. Just wait for it. But for now you're going to have to choose again. But hurry—that flame is upon you, and it burns!

Head back to 216 ●●●●

●●

When Topiasaurus Rex is upon you, you extend the Golden Clippers quickly and bring the blades together, taking a good chunk out of its foot. The creature roars in plant-ish pain and looks down at you in anger. You've hurt it, but not in the right spot, and now it's coming after you again. Try a new move!

Head back to 3 ●

●●●

At the very last moment you lose your nerve and drive the Grass Yacht to the right, hoping to avoid Kirk S.'s rake, but you lose control and head up the slope of the bowl . . . directly toward Kirk E.! Or is it Kirk C.? Whichever Kirk it is, he doesn't see you coming, and you T-bone his fancy lawn mower, turning both of your mowers into hunks of twisted metal. And with no lawn mower to ride, you have to accept that it's now . . .

GAME OVER. CONTINUE: Y/N?

Y: Head to 225 ● N: Head to 248 ●●

Turning the Mow-Luxe to the right, you are met by an impenetrable wall of vegetation that won't yield no matter how hard you push against it. Why? Because your mower isn't running, that's why! You feel a tap on your shoulder and turn around: The snake in the grass is right behind you, its fang-y mouth open wide. Yep . . .

YOU ARE DEAD. CONTINUE: Y/N?

Y: Head to 95 ● N: Head to 248 ●●

●

Hoping to outflank the snake and attack the grass from another angle, you move to the left, but the snake's eyes follow you. This snake won't be fooled. Choose another move.

Head back to 89 ●●

You approach the supine form of Dobermann Pincer, and he's still struggling to right himself, so you have time to choose another move. Choose it now!

Head back to 83 ●●●●

You charge right back at Topiasaurus Rex and end up running toward one of its enormous feet . . . which comes down directly on you, crushing you like a lawn bug. Terrible, really, but . . .

YOU ARE DEAD. CONTINUE: Y/N?

Y: Head to 129 ● N: Head to 248 ●●

●●●●

Frightened by the attack of the topiary monsters, you quickly retreat from the garden and run back to the crossroads in the hedge maze.

Head back to 129 ●

●

The Cyberanha gets sliced in half in midair, thanks to your well-timed one-two kick. Its front and back go flying, clearing the way for you to proceed, and proceed you must—that boulder's gaining on you!

Head to 153 ●●●

●●

You try to use the Grass Yacht's souped-up jumping mechanism to clear the gap left by the sinkhole, and for a moment it looks as though you're going to make it . . . and then it doesn't look like that at all. It's just too large.

YOU ARE DEAD. CONTINUE: Y/N?

Y: Head to 24 ●●● N: Head to 248 ●●

●●●

You try to confuse Kirk S. by crossing over to the left, but he's too quick for you, and he uses his rake to disarm you. Your rake pops out of your hand and lands in front of the Grass Yacht, which reduces it to metal and wood chips almost instantly. It also seems to have damaged the engine of the Grass Yacht, which sputters to a halt.

"Yes!" crows Kirk S. from his seat as he holds his rake aloft victoriously. "In your face, whoever you are!" You hang your head in shame. Not only have you lost the Mow Bowl, it's also . . .

GAME OVER. CONTINUE: Y/N?

Y: Head to 225 ● N: Head to 248 ●●

●●●●

You hit the throttle of the Mow-Luxe, and the mower responds by revving up and tearing itself out of your hands. You gave it too much power, it appears, and now you have nothing with which to defend yourself against the snake, which creeps toward you. It's safe to say that it has become inevitable that . . .

YOU ARE DEAD. CONTINUE: Y/N?

Y: Head to 160 ●●●● N: Head to 248 ●●

●

Taking advantage of Dobermann Pincer's stunned confusion, you sweep his leg, and this time you connect and your blow flips him onto his back!

Head to 83 ●●●●

You and the Mow-Luxe pop up into the air, and the snake mimics your action. Is it making fun of you? At any rate, jumping isn't what's needed here. Try again!

Head back to 92 ●

You run backward, tripping over the edge of the platform and down into the lava. Oh, that's awful. Just a terrible, ironic way to go.

YOU ARE DEAD. CONTINUE: Y/N?

Y: Head to 74 ● N: Head to 248 ●●

●●●●

You decide to retreat from the bridge . . . directly into the path of the rolling boulder, which doesn't so much tear your union asunder as it flattens it into the ground.

YOU ARE DEAD. CONTINUE: Y/N?

Y: Head to 185 ●●●● N: Head to 248 ●●

●

Just as you're about to hit the brick in the middle of the yard, you lift up the Mow-Luxe. It hops over the obstacle just like a skateboarder doing an ollie, and you clear the brick with inches to spare. What timing! Obstruction avoided, you continue mowing like your life depends on it . . . and it might. It just might.

Head to 89 ●●

●●

Sometimes you kick, and sometimes you get licked by a terrible tongue of fire, and this time it's the latter. You really should have tried to avoid it. Just saying . . .

YOU ARE DEAD. CONTINUE: Y/N?

Y: Head to 74 ● N: Head to 248 ●●

●●●

You decide to push ahead, and when the Mow-Luxe rolls over the brick, you hear a horrific clanging noise as the obstacle tears the blades apart. The metal undercarriage then rips itself to pieces, and the machine explodes when its gas tank is pierced by a rogue piece of shrapnel, taking you with it, ending both your summer vacation AND you. Brutal.

YOU ARE DEAD. CONTINUE: Y/N?

Y: Head to 92 ● N: Head to 248 ●●

You push the Mow-Luxe to the left, mowing through the lawn like a hot lawn mower knife through grass butter. Have you forgotten the snake? It hasn't forgotten you, that's for sure, for you can hear it behind you, hissing, getting closer, closer, closer . . . until it strikes, wrapping itself around your feet. You lose your grip on the Mow-Luxe, and it putters off without you, cutting the grass in wild, weird loops as the snake wraps itself around your legs, your torso, and then . . . around your head, which rhymes with . . .

YOU ARE DEAD. CONTINUE: Y/N?

Y: Head to 160 ●●●● N: Head to 248 ●●

●

You decide to retreat from the giant Cyberanha's active attack . . . directly into the path of the oncoming boulder's passive attack! It's . . . not a good scene. Oops!

YOU ARE DEAD. CONTINUE: Y/N?

Y: Head to 84 ● N: Head to 248 ●●

●●

You turn the Grass Yacht's wheel to the right, and the Mechanic shouts, "What do you think you're doing, kid? If that thing had been running, you would have mowed me over. Drive it outta here!"

Head back to 201 ●

You both perform a roundhouse kick on the King Snake Crawler, but your legs are less powerful than your fists, and your blows have no effect on the battle vehicle and bounce off harmlessly. You move back a bit and have time for another move.

Head back to 74 ●

●●●●

Figuring that your best strategy might not be meeting an unknown threat living underneath the country club, you reverse your mow and retreat, heading back toward the safety of the Shed. Whatever's down there, you can meet it later.

Head to 201 ●

●

You punch your fists together, but nothing happens. Checking the readouts on your gloves, you realize that the Fantastic Fist move needs to charge up. Uh-oh. This isn't going to work just yet. Another move!

Head back to 74 ●

●●

Since you don't have a lawn mower, push or riding, at your disposal, this does nothing . . . for now. Heh heh heh . . .

But seriously, do something else.

Head back to 39 ●●

●●●

You pull back on the steering wheel of the Grass Yacht, and the entire front end of the mower jumps into the air and then lands, bouncing a little bit. "I put some hydraulics in there, just in case. For emergencies," says the Mechanic. "But right now? Just drive and mow." Choose another action.

Head back to 201 ●

Using your forward momentum, you grab hands and . . . leap! As the bridge falls from beneath your feet, you fly through the air and barely manage to make it to the edge! But barely is as good as easily. You're safe on the other side of the chasm!

Head to 29 ●●●

●

You try to walk back through the gate, but the vines have somehow grown quickly while your back was turned, and they grip the gate closed. You're trapped in Vineland! Choose another move.

Head back to 39 ●●

●●

Holding the Golden Hedge Clippers in your hand for a moment, you feel their power course through you. You could face any horticultural menace with these, you think. And then you realize you ARE facing a horticultural menace—the topiary monsters are creeping toward you! They're only a foot away—do something!

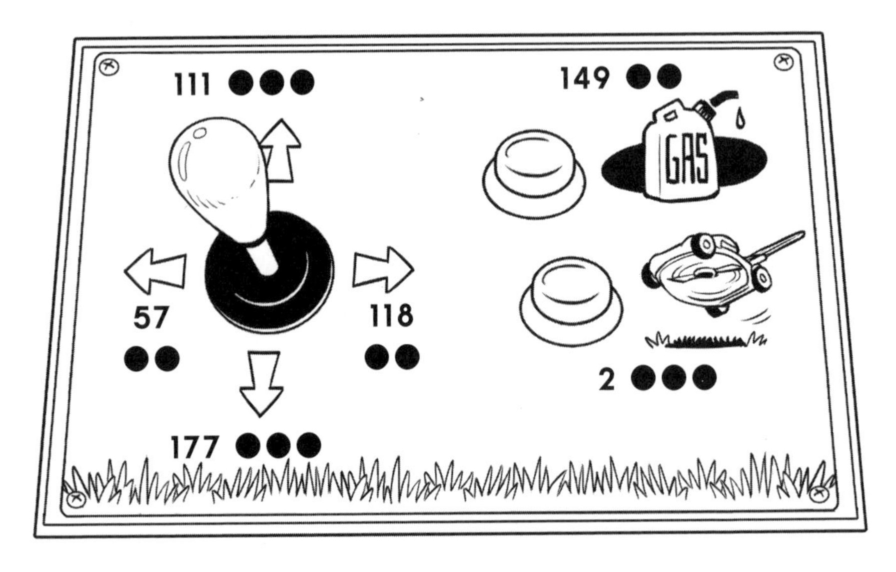

●●●

You punch each other's cybernetic hand, unleashing the power of the Fantastic Fist Bump, but it's TOO MUCH! The boulder is disintegrated and reduced to rubble, but the bridge is also torn apart, sending you down into the raging, Cyberanha-filled waters. As a wise person once said, with great power comes . . . well, you know. Use the Fantastic Fist Bump responsibly! Until you do, though . . .

YOU ARE DEAD. CONTINUE: Y/N?

Y: Head to 185 ●●●● N: Head to 248 ●●

Oddly, you decide to push the Mow-Luxe directly into the front end of the car waiting at the intersection, and the impact puts a significant dent in its hood as well as causing your motor to die. Almost immediately, you're surrounded by the irate driver and Cutter and the other remaining member of the Hedgelordz. This doesn't look good. In fact, it looks like it's . . .

GAME OVER. CONTINUE: Y/N?

Y: Head to 55 ●● N: Head to 248 ●●

You press the Start button at the core of your being, and when you do, you feel your essence hurtling toward the couple at the speed of light, and . . .

. . . you're inside a body! And looking down at yourself, you see that you're dressed up in a sharp-looking jacket and tie. You're the groom!

Shocked at your freaky transition to a new form, you react too slowly to the group of R.A.T. flunkies that blitz and tackle you like a nefarious offensive line. Buried under a pile of them, you watch helplessly as they snatch your bride and bundle her into their waiting helicopter, then take off and zip away toward the horizon. No! You have to save her!

You notice that the wedding band has switched up the music to match the mood at the marred marriage: The sunglasses-wearing keyboard player has flipped a switch on his instrument, changing its tone from CHURCH ORGAN to WICKED SYNTHESIZER, and he leads the rest of the band in a wild, pulsing electronic tune that fills you with adrenaline.

"We call this little electro ditty 'Violent Romance,'" says the keyboard player. "We hope all you F.I.S.T.S. and all you R.A.T. warriors dig it as a soundtrack to your ferocious matrimonial battle. Yeah!"

Energized by the music, you summon up a reserve of strength from deep within, and yelling the words "Fantastic Fist!" and flexing your muscles, you send your assailants flying. When they land on the ground, unconscious, their bodies flash for a moment and then blink away into nothingness. Bizarre.

"Don't worry about those R.A.T. rats," Captain Lu says as he punches another thug, who promptly falls, flashes, and then disappears. "They just re-spawn back at their secret lair and come back again and again and again, like the vermin they are." All around you, it's a free-for-all: The weeping cyborg in a kilt is using his *cromach* (that's a Scottish walking stick) to deliver a sound thrashing to an opponent, and the black and white ninjas are fighting back-to-back against a horde. It's mayhem, but it's kind of . . . awesome.

"Our only hope to save your sweetheart is to get to the other chopper I flew to the wedding. It's parked in the parking lot," says Captain Lu. "I'll run ahead and get it started. You take care of these guys, and I'll meet you there. Got it? Good!"

Not waiting for a response, your commanding officer rushes ahead through the crowd, deftly weaving his way through the throngs toward the distant parking lot. That's where you need to get to if you want to see your sweetheart again, but you don't think you'll have as easy a time as Captain Lu, for the R.A.T. forces are marshaling, and it looks like they will do anything it takes to stop you. You advance on them. It's time to catch some R.A.T.s.

Head to 18 ●●

●●

As the topiary creatures approach, you decide to use the tool in your hand, furiously opening and closing the blades of the Golden Clippers over and over and over, until the topiary creatures are reduced to nothing more than a pile of lawn clippings!

Once the creatures are defeated, the Golden Clippers fade away, disappearing to what you can only assume is some sort of mystic inventory screen somewhere else. You have the feeling that if you need them again, however, they'll be at your disposal. Satisfied, you head back to the crossroads.

Head to 129 ●

●●●

Pistolwhip unleashes a flurry of attacks at you, which you just barely avoid by staying out of her reach. Phew! She slows down and backs up. "What, are you afraid to face me?" she says through a sneer. "So much for the legendary courage of the F.I.S.T.S.!" And then she charges again!

Head back to 195 ●

You move to the right, and Topiasaurus Rex doesn't catch your movement until too late because it doesn't have a head on its left side. You're very smart, and you've bought a few moments. But now it's attacking again, so you must move again!

Head back to 178 ●

●

You move forward toward the R.A.T., and he backs up straight into the pilot, who loses control of the helicopter for a moment. The lurching of the craft causes the copilot and the other R.A.T. to grab handholds, pausing your fight until the pilot can gain control again. Seconds later, you're flying smoothly, so it's time to move.

Head back to 58 ●●●

●●

You move forward, up the path, and head directly toward Vineland, and soon you emerge from the hedge maze. Looking back at it, you can't help but wonder what other secrets might have been hidden there. Still musing, you turn to face the mansion.

Head to 231 ●●●●

You're in the pilot's seat of a helicopter—where do you want to jump to, anyway? Choose another action—that missile is right on your tail!

Head back to 206 ●●

You swerve to the left and juuuuuuust make it around the sinkhole. Phew, that was close!

Head to 36 ●●●●

●

You punch down at Dobermann Pincer, but he rolls over, and your cybernetic glove only strikes sand. And in that moment, he closes a claw around your neck and squeezes until . . .

YOU ARE DEAD. CONTINUE: Y/N?

Y: Head to 169 ● N: Head to 248 ●●

●●

Just as the line in the ground reaches you, you make the Mow-Luxe jump up in the air and let it pass harmlessly beneath you. But you come down on ground that is now unstable. It cracks and then crumbles, sending you and the Mow-Luxe down into a vast underground chasm. Here you see all of the strange creatures that live underneath Lawndon. Troglodytes, dark elves, goblins, kobolds, and . . .

MURRAY.

YOU ARE DEAD. CONTINUE: Y/N?

Y: Head to 10 ●● N: Head to 248 ●●

●●●

You're almost there, almost to the other side of the chasm. The Cyberanhas have returned to their watery home, seemingly sensing that they can't reach you. There are mere yards to go . . . but then, the weight of the boulder finally proves too much of a strain for the bridge, snapping it! You only have a moment to figure out what to do next, and now that moment is OVER! Move!

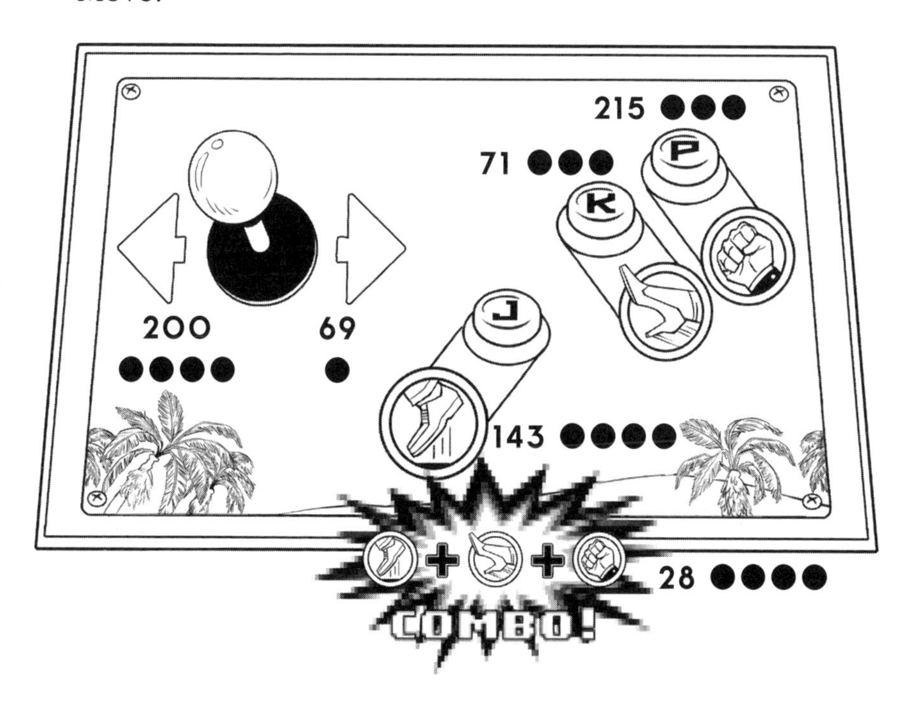

●●●●

The Grass Yacht emerges from the Shed, and although it takes a few moments for you to get used to driving the vehicle, after a few experimental turns and runs, you feel like you've gotten the hang of it, and pretty soon you're cutting the grass on the golf course like you've been doing it for years. The Grass Yacht isn't as deluxe as the lawn mowers the Rakes were riding on, but you can tell that the Mechanic has lovingly maintained this vehicle. In fact, you think that you like it almost as much as your Mow-Luxe!

Soon, your mowing takes you deep into the golf course, way past the ninth hole and out of sight of the clubhouse. You're all alone out here, and as you commence mowing the green you're on, a bowl-like area bordered by the woods on one side and a steep, rounded hill on the other, you begin to wonder: What's up with this level two? Level one was evidence that *MowTown* isn't one of those modern video games where everything is peaceful and relaxing. No, *MowTown* is full of action . . . and something called Murray. But when will the action start up again?

Almost as if on cue, you hear a buzzing sound coming from the direction of the clubhouse. Seconds later, Kirk and his Rakes cronies drive their riding lawn mowers over the crest of the hill, heading directly toward you. Each of them has a fancy-looking rake stored on their lawn mower, like swords in scabbards. They descend into the bowl, circling your position, surrounding you, and you can see that Kirk is speaking to you, moving his mouth and sneering. You shrug. He points at you. You point at your ear—all these engines are too loud. He makes a slashing motion at his throat, and he and the Rakes kill their engines simultaneously, leaving only yours softly running. The Mechanic's done a good job.

"What I was saying," says Kirk from his seat, "is that the other Rakes and I do not appreciate a plebe from the suburbs coming up to OUR country club and telling US how to mow lawns, so we would appreciate it if you would take your hunk-of-junk lawn mower back down the hill and go back to cutting the grass of little old ladies and leave the care and maintenance of a top-flight golf course to the professional elite."

"Bravo, Kirk S.," says one of the other Rakes.

"Indeed, Kirk S.—a rousing speech," says the third.

"Thank you, Kirk E. and Kirk C.," says the lead Kirk. He turns back to you. "So: Are you going to go, or are we, the Rakes, going to be forced to eject you? And believe me, if you choose the latter, it will be messy." Kirk S., Kirk E., and Kirk C. all laugh, pop their collars, and adjust their sunglasses. On the one hand, they outnumber you. But on the other hand, they're jerks. So what do you do?

If you drive the Grass Yacht back to the Shed, head to 100 ●●

If you challenge the Rakes, head to 225 ●

●

Boulder behind and Cyberanhas ahead, you both jump up, letting the boulder pass beneath. At first it seems like a great plan, as the killer fish bounce off the rolling stone harmlessly, clearing your way. But as the rock nears the far end of the bridge, its weight becomes too much for the bridge to bear, and the structure snaps! And that means you both fall down toward the rocks and the Cyberanhas. But at least you're together, right?

YOU ARE DEAD. CONTINUE: Y/N?

Y: Head to 185 ●●●● N: Head to 248 ●●

●●

You look at Cutter, matching his glare with one of your own, then turn to your lawn mower, your hands on its handlebar. You don't move. Behind you, the Hedgelordz laugh. "See?" Cutter says to his lawn flunkies. "I told you this kid was a pushover." And that's when you begin to run, your chugging lawn mower ahead of you, leaving the Hedgelordz behind.

"Hey, kid! You stop right now!" Cutter yells as he and the other Hedgelordz rev up their Scooter Mowers and begin to pursue you. The chase is on! You'd better get to your first job before the Hedgelordz get to you!

Head to 55 ●●

You jam your fists together to make the Fantastic Fist, and it's a spectacular move, its force sending out a wave of crackling energy that halts the boulder's motion, destroys the Cyberanha, and reduces the bridge to nothingness. Everything about this is good, except for the last part. That's bad, because now you're falling to your deaths.

YOU ARE DEAD. CONTINUE: Y/N?

Y: Head to 84 ● N: Head to 248 ●●

You press down the Grass Yacht's gas pedal, and the four-wheeled mowing machine putters its way out of the Shed. As you exit, the Mechanic gives you a thumbs-up.

Head to 154 ●●●●

●

You wade into the crowd of R.A.T. thugs, cracking skulls, shins, and assorted other bones, until all that remains is a moaning pile of broken lackeys, who blink and disappear. This is the best R.A.T. can send? Pathetic. Tossing the crowbar aside, you leave the dance floor.

Head to 229 ●●●

You leap into the air at least a couple of feet. Wow! The exercise you've been getting seems to have paid off. Knowing your gaming tropes, though, you realize this means you'll be needing to jump over, on, or through something soon. Be prepared, and choose another move!

Head back to 39 ●●

●●●

You push the helicopter's controls forward, and the chopper speeds ahead, not far enough to outrun the missile, but far enough that it only takes out your rear rotor . . . which sends your chopper into a scenario of the crash-landing variety!

Head to 49 ●●●

●●●●

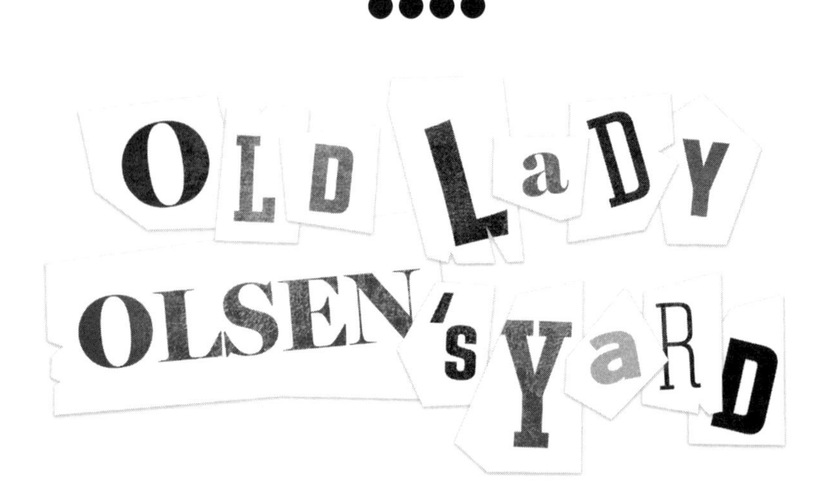

You push the Mow-Luxe to the end of the cul-de-sac and skid to a halt in front of the house directly at the street's head, turning off the engine. It's a tidy little cottage, in front of which stands an old woman who carries a tall, frosty glass of lemonade on a tray. Next to her is her mailbox, upon which the words "Old Lady

Olsen" are painted. You look over your shoulder, just in case Cutter has somehow managed to keep pursuing you, but he's nowhere to be seen. Phew. That takes care of that, at least. But what now?

"I'm so glad you could come over and mow my lawn, you enterprising young whippersnapper," says Old Lady Olsen. "It's gotten . . . a little bit out of hand, I'm ashamed to say." You wipe the sweat from your brow and reach out for the cold drink, but the woman moves it away from your grasp.

"Ah ah ah," she says. "Lemonade's for mowers. You have to get your work done before you get a reward. Follow me."

She turns and walks toward a gate that leads to what you assume is her backyard. You follow, pushing the Mow-Luxe. Once at the gate, she unlatches it and opens it for you. She nods as you pass through, saying, "Remember—once you're done, you get some lemonade, but ONLY when you're done." You turn to ask her if you could possibly have a sip now, as you're REALLY thirsty, but instead she slams the gate shut, trapping you in the backyard! You hear an almost-sinister chuckle from the other side of the gate. "Don't worry, kid. I know the yard's overgrown, but this lemonade is worth it. Trust me!"

You slowly turn around, and as you do, you can hear the sounds of a jungle begin to bubble up. The calls of exotic birds, the hum of bugs, the hissing of strange reptiles—it surrounds you, and you immediately see why: Old Lady Olsen's yard isn't simply a bit messy, it's turned into a wild quarter acre that might as well be in the middle of a rain forest! You have your work cut out for you . . . or at least you will, once you start cutting!

Suddenly, just ahead of you, a snake emerges from the tall grass, its tongue flicking and its fangs glistening with some sort of suburban jungle poison. The time has come to start your first job, so . . .

WHAT DO YOU DO?

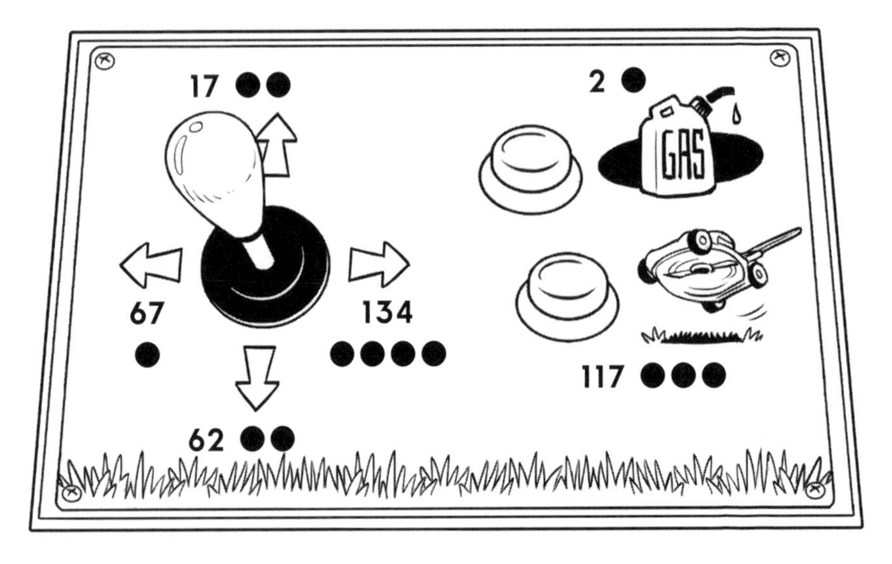

●

As the pistol flashes and the bolt arcs toward you, you throw your cybernetic fist forward, deflecting the projectile directly back at its source. Pistolwhip hisses and drops the weapon as you execute a pretty sweet roll onto the ground and back up again!

Head to 195 ●

●●

You push the Mow-Luxe forward just as the snake makes to strike . . . and at the last moment, it darts into the thick grass. You quickly lose sight of the creature in the underbrush, but no matter: You're cutting a wide swath of Old Lady Olsen's overgrown backyard. Now you're mowing!

Head to 204 ●●●

You shimmy back on the landing skid, and the R.A.T. moves forward toward you, kicking at you but only finding empty air. Move again!

Head back to 94 ●●●●

●●●●

You roll to the left . . . and Topiasaurus Rex tracks your movement, as its last remaining head is on its right side! And sadly, that means that the head has gotten ahold of you and that . . .

YOU ARE DEAD. CONTINUE: Y/N?

Y: Head to 170 ●● N: Head to 248 ●●

●

Timing it just right, you direct a quick one-two jab at the R.A.T. henchman's gut. "Oof!" he says as he falls to his knees and drops his crowbar. His body flashes brightly for a moment and then disappears, but the crowbar stays behind. It flashes as well, and you reach out to grab it, thinking that it might disappear, too, but when you wrap your fingers around it, you find that it's VERY solid and VERY heavy. Aha—that's why R.A.T. uses these things! They'd hurt somebody badly.

Head to 243 ●●●●

●●

You walk up the path a ways and follow it as it twists back and forth. Soon, you've left the gate behind and come to a crossroads, with the path continuing forward and branching off to the left and to the right.

Head to 129 ●

You step forward, directly into Pistolwhip's mighty punch, which sends you spinning and then falling to the ground. As it turns out, she's very good with a pistol, a whip, AND her fist, and as she stands over you, raising her eyebrow mockingly, you think that maybe she should change her code name to Pistolwhipfist. No, that's just stupid. And by the way, it's . . .

GAME OVER. CONTINUE: Y/N?

Y: Head to 3 ●●●● N: Head to 248 ●●

Not only does Kirk S. get under your skin, he seems to know what you're planning to do before you make a decision. You wonder what kind of training the country club must offer.

As Kirk S. gets close, you turn the Grass Yacht to the

right, hoping to avoid him, but he senses your intention and moves to his left. Your mowers scrape against each other in a shower of sparks, and you lose control! The Grass Yacht zooms up the bank of the Mow Bowl and launches into the air toward the woods and into a tree. What a way to mow, er, go. Too bad, kid . . .

YOU ARE DEAD. CONTINUE: Y/N?

Y: Head to 154 ●●●● N: Head to 248 ●●

●

Your punch has stunned Dobermann Pincer, but it looks as if he could recover at any moment. It's time to follow up that punch with something else that could incapacitate him. What else do you have to offer?

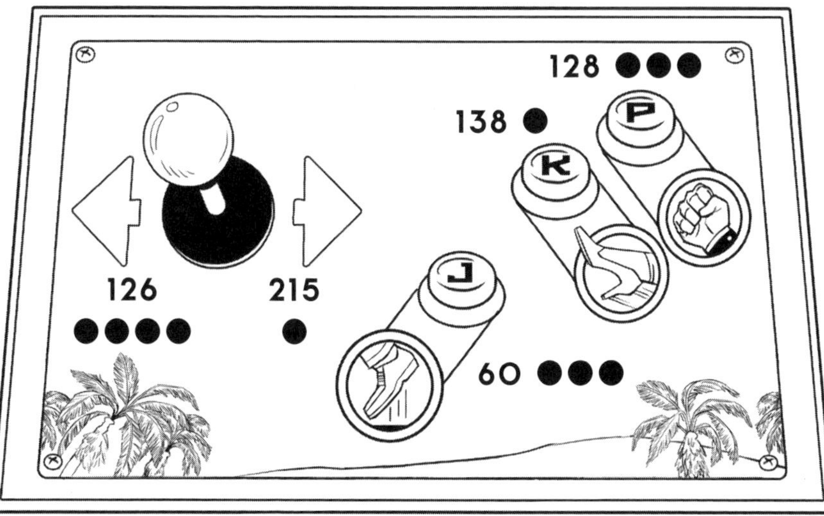

●●

Reeling from the loss of two of its heads, Topiasaurus Rex shakes furiously, a move that dislodges you from its shoulder. You plunge down its body, your hands grasping at stray branches to slow your fall. It works somewhat. But you're battered. Exhausted from all the yard work you've been doing over the course of the long *MowTown* day. If you don't get some refreshment, you don't think you can carry on. But wait—DO you have some lemonade?!

If you found the can of Lawndon's Own Lemonade, head to 178 ●

If you did not find the can of Lawndon's Own Lemonade, head to 114 ●

Just ahead, you can see your destination: R.A.T.'s island lair, complete with volcano at the center. That's where your bride is, and that's where you're going! But as you get closer, you see a rising column of smoke coming from the island's beach. Squinting, you can see the helicopter that took your sweetheart down on the shore below, but . . . it's in pieces and in flames. No! You're too late! Or . . . are you? Just then Captain Lu taps you on the shoulder; using sign language due to the noise of the chopper, he indicates that he's well enough to take over the controls. Nodding, you move aside and let him.

Moments later, Captain Lu is about to land the helicopter on the sands, and you jump from the craft before it touches down, eager to investigate, to know the truth. Blades still whipping around, the wind from them sending your tie and jacket flapping, you walk toward the flaming wreckage of the other vessel, the heat from the wreck giving you a gasoline sunburn. The fire is so intense, there's no way anyone could have survived.

But as you shield your eyes from the blinding glare and devastating warmth, you see something within the military-industrial inferno before you: There's a person in

there! You can see the outline of their body as they slowly emerge from the blaze. Whoever it is, they must be incredibly tough to have survived that crash, so you wipe the blood from your face, the sweat from your brow, and the tears from your eyes and set yourself into a fighting stance, using your F.I.S.T.S. karate and yoga training to steady yourself. Your breath becomes even, and your body bobs up and down in the same cycling, limited motion, as though you are waiting for something in the

game to allow you to advance. The figure in the flames gets closer, until . . . yes! You can finally make out who it is! It's incredible! It's unbelievable. It's . . . the bride.

Have you played as the bride yet?

If no, head to 106 ●

If yes, head to 84 ●

The snake vanquished, you move the Mow-Luxe forward, taking care of the last tuft of unmowed vegetation. That's it—you've conquered Old Lady Olsen's yard! The final blade of grass felled, you let the Mow-Luxe's engine putter and die, and turn to see your handiwork: What was minutes ago an untamed, trackless expanse of backyard is now a neatly mowed patch of land, suitable for backyard barbecues and games of croquet. Good work.

"Oh my!" says Old Lady Olsen as she emerges from her back door, still carrying the tray with the frosty cool glass of lemonade on it. "What a remarkable job you've done. You more than deserve this refreshing cold drink." You reach out to grab the glass, but just as you're about to touch it, a phone rings inside the house, and Old Lady Olsen turns toward the sound. "Pardon me for one moment, would you?" Both she and the tray go back into the house, and you can hear her pick up the phone and talk for a moment. Seconds later, she reemerges into the backyard, phone in her hand. No lemonade. She holds out the receiver to you.

"It's . . . for you," she says, slightly surprised.

You hold the phone to your ear and say a confused hello.

"Hey there, kid. Word's out on you, that you're some sort of hotshot when it comes to this mowing-lawns thing. Well, I've got a job for you. Lawndon Acres Country Club. Edge of town. Now. Can you make it?"

You look at Old Lady Olsen. She shrugs. You shrug back at her. "Well?" says the person on the phone. Figuring that this might be the next level of the game, you tell the person on the other end of the line that you'll be right there. They hang up abruptly, almost before you're finished speaking. Handing the phone back to Old Lady Olsen, you ask if you can have your lemonade now. She scoffs and shakes her head. "Pffft! There's no time for such frosty frippery—you have another job! Go on, off with you!" She shoos you away, and you exit her backyard, pushing the Mow-Luxe before you and headed to your next mowing job / date with destiny.

Head to 10 ●●

●

You push the controls forward, hoping to pick the Flying R.A.T. out of the sky before he completes his mission, but that move only brings you closer to the blast, which incinerates him, you, some passing seabirds . . . basically everything within a radius of a few hundred yards. Ow.

YOU ARE DEAD. CONTINUE: Y/N?

Y: Head to 203 ●● N: Head to 248 ●●

●●

You push the controls forward, causing the chopper to put its nose down and zoom ahead. The blades catch a few unlucky Flying R.A.T.s in the deadly whirl, and well, it's not pretty. But it IS effective! You've cleared out some of your opponents, but many remain!

Head to 203 ●●

You back away from the topiary creatures, retreating from the stone in which the Golden Clippers were embedded. Your escape is only temporary, for you back into the foliage wall of the garden, and the monsters are still coming toward you. Try a new move!

Head back to 144 ●●

Dobermann Pincer crab-walks forward in his exo-suit, claws clacking. "So! We meet on the field of bat—" he begins, but you two interrupt him with a double kick, a chorus line of pain! His armor takes the brunt of the damage, though, and he and Pistolwhip remain there, ready to go again. Choose another move!

Head back to 29 ●●●

•

You think of the can of Lawndon's Own that you found earlier, and you pull it from your back pocket where you originally stashed it, and somehow it's still ice-cold! You open it and chug it down, its sweet, lemony goodness spreading a feeling of well-being and cool refreshment throughout your body. Once done, you toss the can away.

You're full of lemonade.

It's time to finish the ultimate lawn-care job.

And then, as if on cue, Topiasaurus Rex strikes, its remaining head advancing toward you!

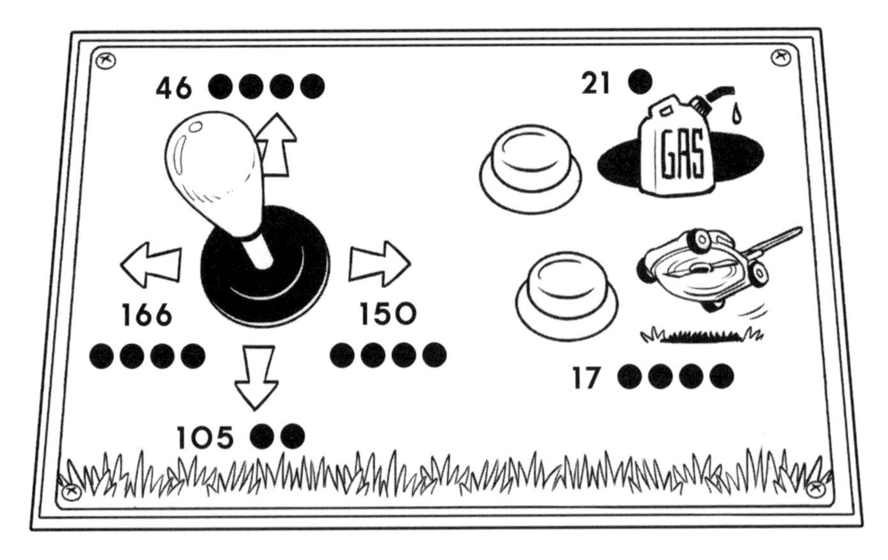

••

The battle over and Dobermann Pincer gone to who knows where, you stand in the glow of the fire of the crashed helicopter, its unearthly heat nothing more than pleasant warmth on your cybernetic skin. You are still, save for your steady breathing. In, out. In, out. If this were a video game, it would be your character's idle animation. Wait a second . . .

Instinctually, without realizing it but perhaps owing to your newly discovered cyborg abilities, you mutter the word "chopper" under your breath, and only then do you hear it: the sound of helicopter blades from off in the distance. Turning, you see a whirlybird approaching the beach on the far side of the twisted metal and dancing flames that used to be the vehicle of your R.A.T. kidnappers.

The new arrival descends toward the beach, but before it can even touch the ground, someone leaps from its side door and proceeds to walk in your direction. Is this another enemy to fight? You look down at your cybernetic battle glove and bring the fingers together in a mighty fist. If so, they'll have to face and be defeated by you. Deciding to make the most epic bridal entrance ever, you stride forward THROUGH the burning wreck, letting the fire singe the edges of your armor-enhanced wedding dress and swirl harmlessly around your cybernetic body. If this doesn't intimidate them, nothing will.

You begin to emerge from the fire, and through the smoke and haze you can almost make out the features of your company. They're shielding their eyes from the brightness around you, but . . . yes. You can see them; you can see their face! It's someone you know! It's . . . the groom!

Have you played as the groom yet?

If no, head to 146 ●

If yes, head to 84 ●

•••

You feel that you're missing . . . something in your room. Something vital that you can use for whatever lies ahead. You give your room another once-over, this time looking closely for anything that could help you.

At first nothing pops out at you. Nothing seems important. But as you shuffle around some things on your desk, you uncover a sheaf of papers that you strangely recognize, even though you've never seen them before! One of them is a map of a seven-block area, with the letter "X" marked on what looks to be an important spot. The other papers are handbills with your face on them, advertisements for your personal lawn-care business. That's it! You know what your game backstory is: You put up these flyers around the neighborhood, and the map shows the location of your first job. YES!

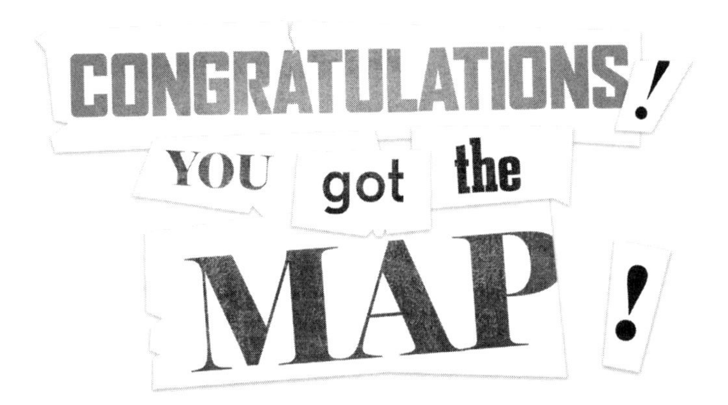

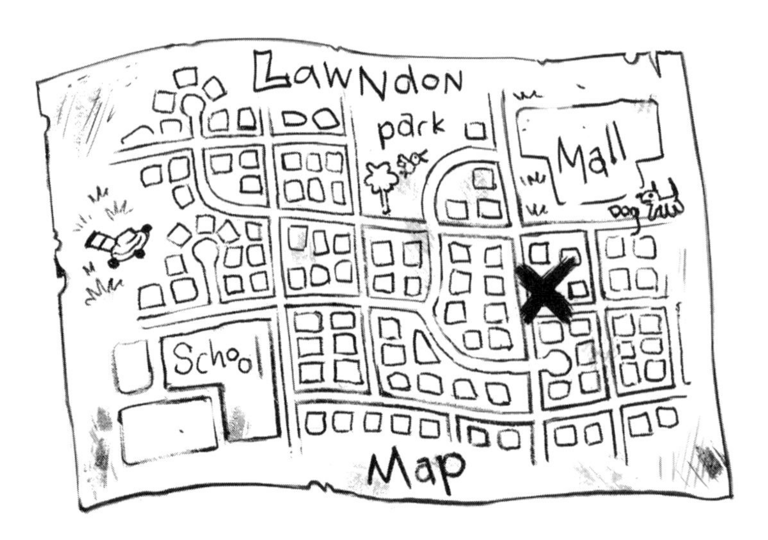

With the map in hand, you feel like you've just taken the first step in the right direction to playing—and winning—this game. You need to get yourself over to the location marked on the map and get to work. That resolved, you decide that it's time to venture out into the world of MowTown, so you turn your back on your room, slip out of your open window, and step outside.

The first thing you notice when you get outside is that the temperature is PERFECT; it's not so hot as to be uncomfortable, but it is warm enough that your skin feels pleasantly toasty. The sun shines brightly up in the sky as clouds drift pleasantly by and occasionally provide some shade. The sound of buzzing is in the air, as honeybees and other insects fly, jump, and crawl around, doing insect-y things. And the smell of grass, flowers, and sprinklers is everywhere, giving the air a natural, earthy aroma. Lawndon—MowTown—feels like the place where summer begins and ends. In fact, it doesn't feel LIKE summer, it feels like it IS summer—the ULTIMATE summer. Cool. Or, rather, comfortingly warm.

You also notice that the lawn you're standing on—your lawn—has grown tall and wild. Looking up and down the pleasant suburban block you're on, you can see that every other lawn is in basically the same state, and that there are a few people—some by themselves, some in small crews—getting an early start on making deals with the residents to take care of their greenery. You figure that you should be doing the same thing, but you realize that you're lacking an important element in your endeavors, namely something to cut grass with! Everybody else on the street has their preferred tool;

some have old-fashioned push mowers, some have gas-powered ones, but every one of them is unique, like their owners have spent hours customizing and improving them to their personal satisfaction.

You walk the perimeter of your house, hoping to find something you can use to get into the lawn game. Moments later, you come to your garage, its door open. And before you is a machine that you recognize, even though you've never seen it before—it's your personal lawn mower, a vintage Mow-Luxe 2000 push mower, gas-driven. A little banged up but trusty. Solid.

Head to 8 ●●●●

It sounds like the most epic brawl EVER is happening inside the *Fantastic Fist* machine, so you find yourself edging closer to it to see what sort of mayhem is going on. Token at the ready, you let it fall into the coin slot with a satisfying *CHA-CHUNK*.

You press the Player 1 button, and a voice growls, "Fantastic FIST! YEAH!" from inside the machine, the bass in its speakers turned up so high, you can feel it in your chest. A gust of wind blows your hair back, and the screen glows so bright, you can't help but close your eyes for a moment. When you open them, you're no longer in the Midnight Arcade—instead, you're standing behind a crowd gathered on a beautiful seaside cliff. Glancing around, you see that everybody in the audience is dressed in formal wear, looking at a bride and groom standing near the cliff. Both of them look pretty tough, like they work out, but not too much. They look dangerous and ready to fight. Between the couple stands a handsome, middle-aged man with gray hair at his temples, a mustache, and an eye patch. He is talking to the audience.

"We are gathered here today to celebrate the union between these two special individuals," he says, his

gravelly voice carrying all the way back to where you are, disembodied. "Two people who found each other through work, and through work, found love. As you all know, their work is kicking butt as members of the F.I.S.T.S., the Fighting Initiative for Stopping Terrible Stuff . . ."

At the mention of the F.I.S.T.S., the assembled crowd cheers, and you can see that everybody in attendance also looks similarly muscular and fit, as if they are all ready for a fight at any moment. Everyone is dressed in unique and semi-outlandish formal wear, and each individual's choice of clothes seems to reflect some sort of technical specialty. There's a white-masked ninja in a white suit holding hands with a black-masked ninja in a black dress, and on the other side of the aisle, what looks to be a cyborg in a kilt is dabbing tears from its eyes. You get it—these are other members of the F.I.S.T.S. who have come to see two of their own get hitched! The man continues speaking.

"You all know me—I'm Captain Lu, their commanding officer, and it's my honor to have been asked to join them together in this civil, nondenominational ceremony. And now, without further ado, may I have the gloves?"

At his request, a small boy approaches, carrying a large pillow upon which rest two matching cybernetic gloves. They look complicated . . . and deadly. Captain Lu holds them up.

"These two cybernetic power gauntlets not only represent an upgrade in these two individuals' ability to fight Terrible Stuff, they represent an upgrade in their relationship. Now, if no one has any objections . . ."

Almost as if on cue, the background organ music is interrupted by the sound of chopper blades, and a helicopter rises behind the bride, groom, and Captain Lu. The door on the side of the copter opens, and a group of mean-looking paramilitary types in goofy uniforms jumps out.

"Greetings, F.A.R.T.S.!" the leader says to the crowd, and you can hear the sarcastic acronym in his tone. "And congratulations from the forces of R.A.T., the Rotten Army of Tyranny!"

It's chaos! The assembled members of F.I.S.T.S. mill about in confusion, and as you look back at the groom, you notice that he has grabbed his cybernetic glove. Above him is an arrow floating in the air pointing down at his head, and he's outlined by a subtle glow. You shift your gaze to the bride, who has also grabbed her cybernetic glove. The arrow moves to float over her, and now SHE'S outlined in the glow. Each time your gaze shifts, the arrow moves to that person. You know what this is—it's a character selection prompt! So, who do you want to play?

If you want to play the groom,

head to 146 ●

If you want to play the bride,

head to 106 ●

●

You hop up in your seat, but that's it. This move does nothing in the helicopter. Choose another move.

Head back to 54 ●

●●

You and the reptile face off . . . and then charge at each other! At the last moment, you gun the engine of the Mow-Luxe, and when you do, the reptile is dragged underneath your lawn mower, its body disappearing in the undercarriage and into the Mow-Luxe's whirring blades. The machine protests for a moment as it chews up the poisonous predator, but the noise subsides almost as quickly as it began.

Head to 174 ●●●●

●●●

You rush ahead . . . directly into Pistolwhip's pistol fire. Oh boy was that unwise. Bad tactics all around. No high score for you in this game, and that's because . . .

YOU ARE DEAD. CONTINUE: Y/N?

Y: Head to 229 ●●● N: Head to 248 ●●

●●●●

You hang a right and manage to avoid the brick, and descend back into the jungle that is Old Lady Olsen's yard. After another right, a left, a left, a right, a left, and another left, you find yourself once again headed straight toward the brick! Choose again, kid.

Head back to 204 ●●●

●

You back up, but there's not much room to move in this cramped space, and the R.A.T. flunky is approaching. Choose again!

Head back to 58 ●●●

●●

You move your mower to the left and let whatever's digging underneath the golf course pass you by. And it does . . . for a moment. Then the line of disturbed earth makes a turn—a U-turn!—and heads right back toward you! Before you can react, the ground beneath your feet crumbles, and you fall into an abyss beneath Lawndon Acres. Yes . . .

YOU ARE DEAD. CONTINUE: Y/N?

Y: Head to 10 ●● N: Head to 248 ●●

You rush toward Pistolwhip just as she makes a wide arc with her whip, which wraps around your body tightly. Thousands of volts of electricity course through its tendril and into your body, and you fall to the ground, smoldering in your suit. You didn't even get any wedding cake, and now . . .

YOU ARE DEAD. CONTINUE: Y/N?

Y: Head to 243 ●●●● N: Head to 248 ●●

You approach the *MowTown* machine, drawn to the gentle music and sound effects pulsating from the cabinet—the tune it plays is a groovy, low-key summer jam that seems to promise hot, sunny days filled with barbecues and mischief, and you think that you can hear, buried in the background noise, the hissing of a sprinkler on a lawn. It sounds peaceful, relaxing, inviting, so you decide to drop the token into its coin slot and see what the game has to offer.

As soon as you do, a new sound overwhelms the music—the sound of a lawn mower starting up! Actually, it suffers from a few false starts, like someone is trying to pull its cord and isn't quite getting it going, but it revs to life quickly, and someone guns the throttle, filling the Midnight Arcade with the smell of gasoline. But . . . how? Games don't have SMELL effects, do they?

Looking at the screen, you see that a new graphic has appeared. Digital clouds part, revealing what looks to be a pleasant small town in the predawn, a bucolic village with its homes surrounded by green spaces of all types—front yards, backyards, parks, and more. The game's camera zooms in, and you can see, on the edge of town, a vast golf course, and even farther beyond that, an enormous mansion surrounded by hedges. Then, a digital sun begins to rise behind the mountains, making the screen brighter and brighter, so bright that you have to close your eyes against the glare even as you hold on tightly to the game's controls. The sound of the lawn mower gets even louder, and a new smell fills your nostrils: the organic perfume of freshly cut grass! Then, bizarrely, you feel yourself begin to fall INTO the screen, directly toward the town below . . .

. . . and then *BAM!* Your fall ends, and you find yourself sitting bolt upright in a bed as a radio next to you on a nightstand comes to life, obviously set as an alarm, and a disc jockey starts talking.

"Gooooooooooood morning, Lawndon! It's eight o'clock in the a.m., and I wanna be the first to welcome you to the first day of summer vacation, aka the BIGGEST holiday in town, also aka the beginning of our fair city's competitive lawn-care season! Can I get a heck yeah? Heck yeah! Word on the street is that the rival lawn-care crews are already roaming around, aiming to get the prime jobs and hoping to become the rulers of the grasslands. Do you have what it takes to be the top lawn ranger in town? The only way you'll know is if you get outta bed and get mowing! With that in mind, here's a little tune to gas up your mower, a funky bit of sunshine soul written about our hometown. That's right! Here's the classic group Push and the Blades with . . . 'MowTown'!"

As the music starts—and yes, it IS pretty funky—you look around what you know is your bedroom in your home in the town you were just somehow falling toward. Lawndon? Is that what the guy on the radio said? And what was that about "competitive lawn-care season"? Bizarre. Figuring that you'll never understand what is going on from the confines of your bed, you pull aside your covers and see that you're not even wearing pajamas—in fact, you're already dressed for a summer day, wearing sneakers, shorts, and a well-worn T-shirt, topped off with a baseball cap to shield your eyes from the sun. You get up and see that your bedroom window is open, letting in warm yellow sunshine, a nice breeze, and the distant sound of lawn mowers starting up.

And that's when it hits you—you know why you're here: You're here to mow lawns, and somehow, you've got to figure out how to become the top lawn jockey in town. Because when you do THAT, that's when you'll get back to the Midnight Arcade and back home.

So what do you do?

If you look out your window, head to 78 ●

If you investigate your room first, head to 42 ●●●●

●

You are face-to-face with Pistolwhip, and she settles into a fighting stance to match yours. "Despite my name, I need neither pistol nor whip to crush you," Pistolwhip says. You raise your eyebrow mockingly. "Oh! A mocking eyebrow? Let's fight in hand-to-hand combat, and then we'll see whose eyebrow will be raised!"

This is it, you think as Pistolwhip tenses for her attack. Your next move will either get you to the chopper . . . or get you dead!

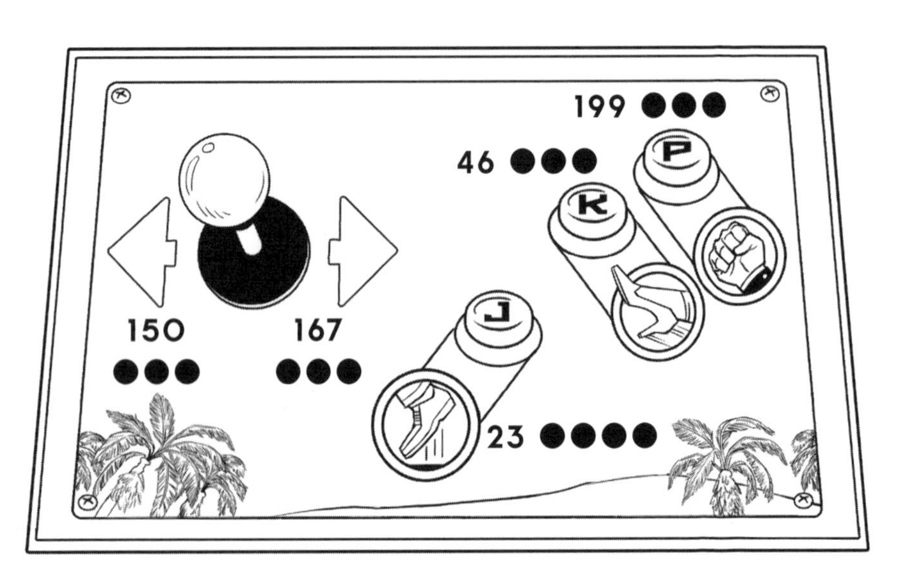

●●

You hit the gas on the Mow-Luxe, and the machine lurches forward with a burst of speed, seemingly impelled by an intelligence of its own to ignore the stop sign. The Hedgelordz follow you into the intersection, and the sound of furious honking and screeching brakes fills the air—you all have mowed right into the path of an oncoming car! Luckily, your speed allows you to narrowly avoid it, but one member of the Hedgelordz isn't so fortunate and gets sent flying into a nearby well-manicured hedge by their impact with the front bumper. You and your lawn mower continue your mad dash down the road, and for a moment you think you're in the clear, but when you glance behind you, you see the remaining two Hedgelordz maneuver their mini-mowers around the stopped car and its yelling driver and accelerate. They're still after you!

Head to 103 ●●●●

●●●

You deliver a roundhouse kick to the R.A.T. henchman's jaw, sending him flying backward into a row of white folding chairs. His prone body blinks rapidly, as does his crowbar, but before you can investigate, both disappear.

Head to 243 ●●●●

The Mow-Luxe hops over a manhole in the middle of the street, but otherwise, this move does nothing. Choose again!

Head back to 103 ●●●●

●

You just made it to the top of the King Snake Crawler and you decide to hop off? Where's the gaming logic in that? Go back to the last move.

Head back to 237 ●

●●

You decide to press the button on the Grass Yacht's dashboard that looks like the throttle on your Mow-Luxe, and when you do, a STREAM OF FIRE erupts from the front of the lawn mower! Kirk S. squeals and turns his lawn mower to the side, barely avoiding the flames. You both end up at opposite ends of the Mow Bowl, facing each other again. "Fight with honor, peasant," he says. "Rakes are the only weapons allowed in the Mow Bowl!" He fixes you with a cruel stare as he drives his lawn mower your way again! Choose another move!

Head back to 225 ●

You throw your mightiest punch at Pistolwhip, but she ducks to the side, allowing your fist to pass harmlessly by her head. And as that happens, she brings up HER fist, which connects to your chin not-so-harmlessly, sending you backward into the air in some sort of video-enhanced, stuttering slow motion. While in the air, you have time to think about what you would have done differently if given a second chance. After what seems like an eternity, you come crashing down to the ground, defeated, and even though you can't see it, you can feel that Pistolwhip is raising her eyebrow at you with maximum mockery.

GAME OVER. CONTINUE: Y/N?

Y: Head to 3 ●●●● N: Head to 248 ●●

●●●●

That's just a terrible, terrible move. You knew it before you made it. What was it, a nervous twitch? No matter.

YOU ARE DEAD. CONTINUE: Y/N?

Y: Head to 101 ●●●● N: Head to 248 ●●

•

Intrigued—and a little scared, to be honest—you decide to enter the Shed and find out more about what the Mechanic was talking about. When you pass through the doors, you see that the Mechanic is crouched near another riding lawn mower, working on it with an assortment of tools.

"Thought you'd want to know what you're getting yourself into, kid," says the Mechanic without turning around. "Murray showed up about a week ago. Don't know where from, don't know how. But he's wrecking the course and making it impossible to golf. The Rakes—those snotty kids on those fancy ridin' mowers—they've got the groundskeeping contract through their connections at the club, but they can't do nothin' about Murray. They think they're so cool. Bah!" The Mechanic spits on the ground and turns to you, shaking a wrench in your direction. "That's why Rodney called you. But you ain't gonna mow the grass and defeat Murray pushing that old Mow-Luxe, however fine a machine it is. You need to upgrade, my friend. To this." He stands aside to reveal the riding lawn mower he's been working on. It's a Mow-Luxe Grass Yacht, an older riding mower, much less ornate than the ones the Rakes are riding, but a classic. "I've made some personal modifications on it. Go ahead, get on."

Reluctantly you let go of your Mow-Luxe's handlebar, but you feel the pull of the Grass Yacht. Sitting in its seat and taking hold of its controls, you immediately feel a connection. YES.

"You control this thing basically the same way you control your old Mow-Luxe," says the Mechanic, pushing your lawn mower to the side. "Don't worry, I'll keep it safe while you go deal with the grass"—he pauses for a moment, looks around—"and Murray," he finishes, his voice low. "Now, go. You can do it, kid!"

The Grass Yacht is pointed toward the exit of the Shed. Where do you want to go?

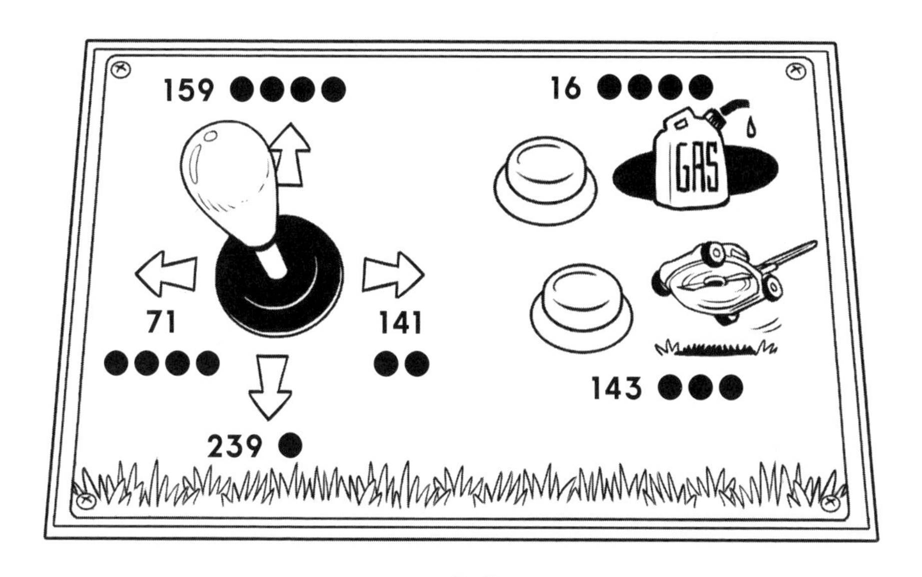

●●

The Flying R.A.T. ahead of you launches a portable missile, and it looks like it's headed directly at your cockpit. Move! Now!

112 ●●●●
122 ●●
P
K
96 ●●
38 ●
J
239 ●●

You're cutting a path through Old Lady Olsen's gnarly junglelike backyard, making progress, when you spot something ahead of you: A piece of brick is jutting up from the ground and is in your way. What's your move?

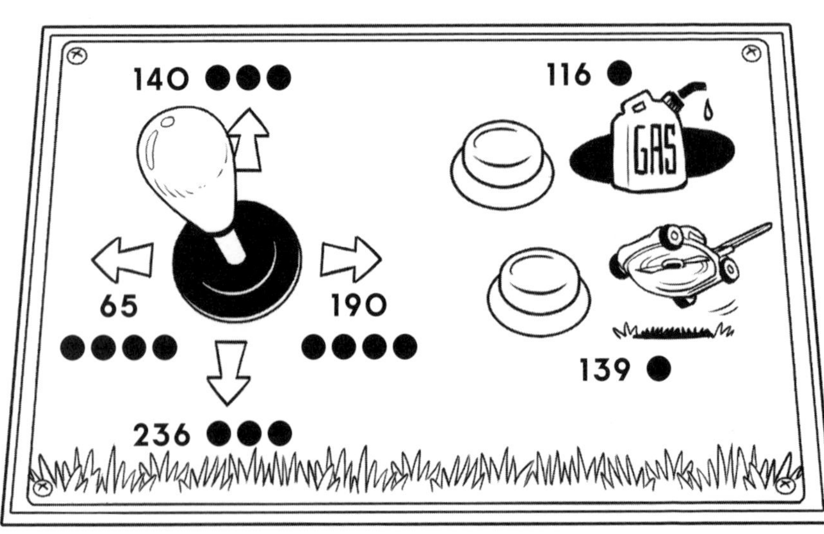

●●●●

Have you earned the crowbar in this game yet? You would know because you would have seen a cool image of one and been told you earned it.

If no, head to 82 ●●

If yes, head to 159 ●

●

That way leads back to the gate to the estate. When you get there, the gate is closed tight by vines. It's not going to work, kid. Go back to the intersection and choose another direction.

Head back to 129 ●

●●

Despite the wildness of its flight, you've been able to stay firmly stuck to the helicopter's landing skid, and now you pull yourself up, figuring that you might as well attempt to pilot this thing. Managing to make it to the pilot's seat, you steady the chopper as it flies over the water, closing in on the volcanic island in the distance. But then, another R.A.T. chopper approaches from behind . . . and it shoots a missile aimed directly at your craft. What are you going to do?

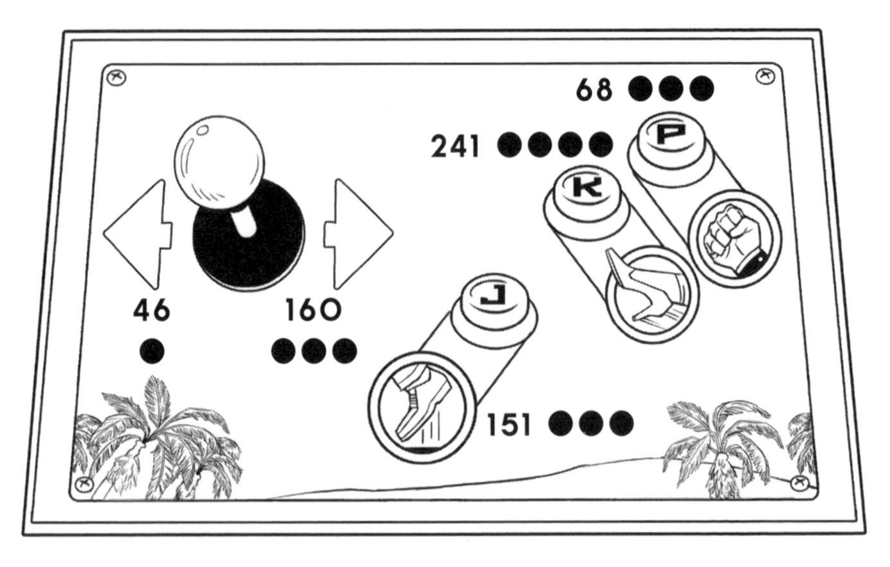

●●●

You exit the garage with your purring Mow-Luxe, emerging into the sweet summer sunshine of Lawndon. Your senses are sharper than you've ever felt them before; you even think you can hear the hum of the grass growing. It's crazy, but you feel like some sort of minor lawn-mowing superhero! It's a good vibe.

You bring the lawn mower to the center of your street and turn to face the horizon. You flex your fingers on the lawn mower's handlebar, and the engine roars. The suburb is open to you. If there ever was a time to cut some grass, it's now. What do you—

"Hey, kid!"

Just as you are about to make a decision as to where to push your mower, a sneering, snotty voice interrupts your train of thought. Looking behind you, you see a trio of teenagers approaching, riding what appear to be motorized scooters. Each of them has their hair cut in a haphazard, messy fashion and wears a jumpsuit with the sleeves ripped off and a name tag sewn to the left chest. They also wear rakes strapped to their backs, the lawn-care tools slung over their shoulders as if they were swords.

CUTTER

You point to your chest. Are they talking to you? They come to a skidding halt directly in front of you, and their sunglasses-wearing leader (his name tag says CUTTER) rudely gets right in your face and holds up a crumpled bit of paper. It's one of your flyers!

"Yeah, kid. I was talking to you. This is you on this piece of trash, isn't it? What do you think you're doing with these flyers and that hunk of junk? Don'tcha know that this neighborhood is Hedgelordz territory?"

At this, all three of the teenagers draw their rakes, turn around, and point to their backs, across which the words THE HEDGELORDZ are stitched. You look closer at their scooters—what you assumed were standard two-wheeled transportation are actually miniature gas-powered lawn mowers. You get it—they're a gang of lawn-mowing punks . . . and apparently you're on their turf!

Cutter turns back around and pokes his rake at you in a menacing fashion, forcing you to back up. "I'm gonna give you a choice here: Take that toy back into your garage, go inside, and leave the lawn care to the professionals. It's either that or watch us Hedgelordz turn it into spare parts right here in the middle of the road. What's it gonna be, huh?"

You turn away from the Hedgelordz and face the

stretch of road and lawns in front of you. The lawn punks are right behind you, breathing down your neck.

WHAT DO YOU DO?

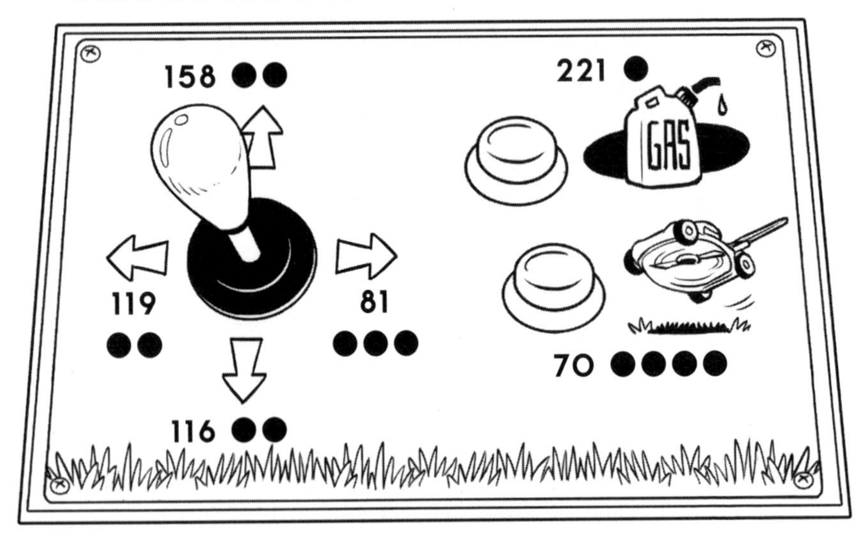

●●●●

This is it. The opportunity you've been waiting for. The Fantastic Fist is charged and ready, and it's the perfect time for a spectacular finishing move, so you and your partner lock gazes and swing hard, your cybernetic fists colliding with incredible force. The resulting wave of power UTTERLY DISINTEGRATES the R.A.T. Hole and tears the King Snake Crawler to pieces, knocking King Snake out in the process. That's it. You did it! You destroyed R.A.T., er, S.N.A.K.E.! Heck yeah!

Head to 218 ●●●●

●

You turn your back on the Shed and head toward the golf greens. After all, you've got your trusty Mow-Luxe and your wits, and you've already defeated the Hedgelordz and conquered Old Lady Olsen's hellscape of a yard. What could possibly stop you now?

Soon, you're on the green and, motor running on the Mow-Luxe, you're busy shaping up the grass and getting it down to regulation, golf-playing length. Compared to what you just went through, Lawndon Acres is a breeze, a real walk in the park (or country club). *If this is a video game*, you think, *this must be a cut-scene before the REAL challenge*.

As if in answer to your thought, the ground shakes. Was that an earthquake? Whatever it was, it's already over. Shrugging, you continue working, but moments later you feel the ground shake again, and this time it continues. Looking out over the smooth grass, you can see that the ground has been disturbed, like something underneath the grass was digging and making the earth buckle. Then, the ground starts cracking, the grass being pushed up and aside in a straight line that's coming toward you, fast! What do you do?!

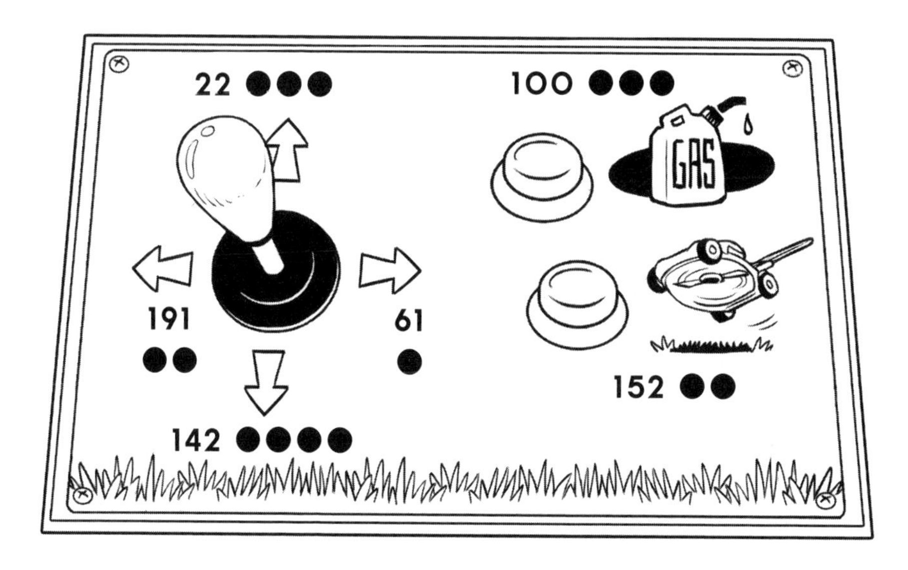

●●

You leap into the air and come down on Dobermann Pincer's chest, cracking open his armor as if you were trying to get at a good bit of crabmeat! You hop off, knowing that your opponent has been vanquished, and when you do, his body flashes a couple of times and then . . . disappears, like defeated enemies do in games like this. So, so strange.

Head to 179 ●●

Just as Murray's about to drive into the Grass Yacht, you activate its special hydraulics, and that allows you to effectively use the berm that Murray's digging is making as an improvised ramp! You fly through the air and then—*BAM!* Land safely! Epic move, kid, but keep going. You're not out of the woods—or off the green—yet!

Head to 115 ●●●●

Pistolwhip's whip cracks at your feet as you jump out of its reach, sending out sparks and flashes of light. You can smell burning ozone, but you've avoided death . . . for now! Choose again!

Head back to 229 ●●●

●

You move forward, nudging Dobermann Pincer back. He stumbles but doesn't fall. Choose again!

Head back to 169 ●

●●

As you enter the intersection, you sense that there's something wrong—there's a car headed right for you! You try to make the Mow-Luxe hop over the oncoming object, but . . . a lawn mower jumping over a car? We'll spare you the terrible details, but . . .

YOUR LAWNMOWER IS DEAD. CONTINUE: Y/N?

Y: Head to 207 ●●● N: Head to 248 ●●

●●●

You punch the empty air in front of you, but all that does is ensure that you go down swinging. Get it? You're falling down. Into a canyon. Eh?

YOU ARE DEAD. CONTINUE: Y/N?

Y: Head to 101 ●●●● N: Head to 248 ●●

King Snake snarls. “You think your pitiful punches can stop the slithering of S.N.A.K.E.? Think again!” With that, he presses another button, and a plume of fire shoots from the front of the King Snake Crawler. Take action!

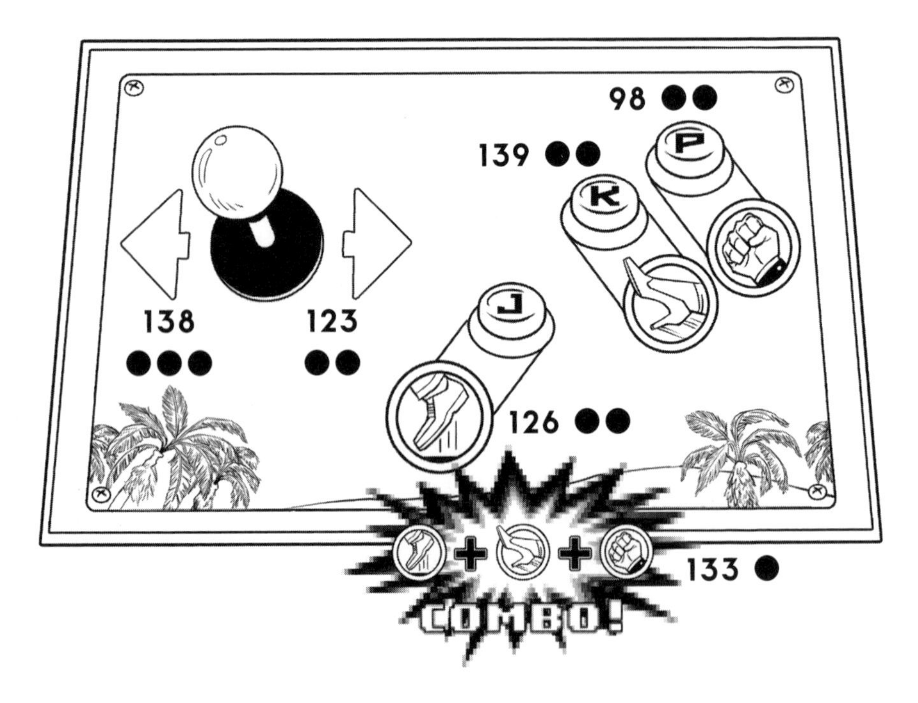

●

Your reflexes have been honed to catlike levels from years of observing all the cats that hang around at F.I.S.T.S. headquarters, so it's no problem to jump over Pistolwhip's blast . . . for now. Choose another move!

Head back to 3 ●●●●

Just as you and Kirk S. are about to cross rakes, you activate the Grass Yacht's jumping mechanism, coming down on the front end of Kirk S.'s lawn mower, the impact of which sends both him and his rake flying over your head. He hits the ground behind you, rolls, and comes to a stop, sitting on his butt and looking dazed.

Head to 24 ●●●

You sweep your leg toward Dobermann Pincer's feet, but he jumps up nimbly, avoiding your strike. Choose again!

Head back to 49 ●●●

The battle is over, and King Snake lies in what used to be the King Snake Crawler, completely unconscious. You and your betrothed look at each other—this would have been impossible without both of you, and even though it's your wedding day, it's you who have given the gift, a gift to the world—freedom from the tyranny of a megalomaniacal villain with indefinite goals. You gently tap your cybernetic fists together, and as you do, applause erupts from behind you. Turning, you see you have an audience: It's Captain Lu!

Captain Lu approaches and snaps off a jaunty salute. "I bet you're wondering why I left you two on the beach back there." You both nod. Yes, you are. "Well, it's because I knew you could handle this army all by yourselves. You didn't need me or my heavily armed helicopter; you only needed each other."

You both crease your eyebrows at the other, not quite agreeing with the captain's logic but going along for the sake of it.

"I also wanted to go get some . . . reinforcements, so to speak. Of the romantic variety."

He whistles, and a crowd of people begin to enter the volcano lair: It's your wedding guests, which are made up of 15 percent family and friends and 85 percent members of F.I.S.T.S.!

Everybody's here, the entire roll call of the membership of F.I.S.T.S.: Killer B. Kilt, the Highlander Cyborg; Shadow and Light, the black-and-white ninja couple; Zapp, Cameo, Brainstorm, K-Doe, Brick, Hip-Drop, Switch, Dazz, S.O.S. . . . even obscure but essential members like Blackrock and Yellow Sunshine are there, and they all came for you. They applaud heartily until Captain Lu motions for silence.

"We took care of the rest of the R.A.T.s as we came in, so there won't be any further interruptions," he says. "And now that your dearly beloved are gathered here today in this volcano lair, why don't we have ourselves a wedding?"

The assembled crowd cheers again, but the celebration is interrupted by Killer B. Kilt, who points behind you.

"Och! That schnake is gettin' away!" he shouts in his robotic brogue. Everyone turns to look, and it's true—King Snake has revived and activated an escape pod on his vehicle!

"This isn't over yet, F.I.S.T.S., not by a long shot," he cries as his throne rises from the scraps of the King Snake

Crawler, up toward the crater of the volcano. "I will rebuild, and S.N.A.K.E. shall slither again in *Fantastic Fist 2*! And by the way: Congratulations! You make a beautiful and deadly couple!" And then he's gone.

"We'll deal with him later," says Captain Lu. "Now, it's time for cake!"

Once again, the chip-tune "Wedding March" plays, and this time everyone starts dancing, the floor of the volcano lair making a natural dance floor. You've beaten *Fantastic Fist*! So . . . what now?

If you want to play *MowTown*, head to 192 ●●●●

If you've beaten both games, head to 248 ●●

●

You defiantly squeeze the throttle on the Mow-Luxe, and its engine roars, sending out a cloud of black smoke and causing the Hedgelordz to reflexively jump back in awe. They look at you warily for a moment, then creep back toward you.

Try another move!

Head back to 207 ●●●

From either side, your fists rain down on the head of King Snake, but he is stubbornly still trying to press that button. You've got to choose a more effective, more FINAL move.

Head back to 56 ●●●

You back away from the head and walk backward into empty air. Wow, that was clumsy. And now . . .

YOU ARE DEAD. CONTINUE: Y/N?

Y: Head to 3 ● N: Head to 248 ●●

Pistolwhip defeated, you leap over her prone body as it flashes briefly, then disappears. Weird video game stuff. When you finally make it to the chopper, Captain Lu takes it off the ground almost before you're even safely inside, such is the urgency.

"I'm tracking those R.A.T. finks as we speak," he says, bringing the chopper around and heading over the former site of your wedding and out to sea. "The chopper that took your bride is on a course for R.A.T.'s island lair, just a few clicks off the coast." Looking through the chopper's cockpit window, you can see the plume of smoke coming from the volcano at the center of the island that is home to R.A.T., and you make a mental note to ask, should you ever get out of this, why the designer of *Fantastic Fist* chose to place the site of the heroes' wedding so close to the base of their archenemies.

". . . they're way ahead of us," Captain Lu continues as you tune back in to the conversation. "And we've gotta fight through some enemy ships if we want to go there. Are you with me?"

You give Captain Lu a thumbs-up, and as you do, an explosion rocks your chopper—R.A.T. choppers are dead ahead, and they're coming straight at you! You

look at Captain Lu, but he's been knocked out cold by the impact. Taking immediate action, you push him out of the pilot's seat and take the controls of the chopper yourself. Ahead lies the island of R.A.T., and the only thing keeping you from getting there is the squad of Flying R.A.T.s (R.A.T. thugs wearing helicopter backpacks equipped with rocket launchers and lasers) zooming toward you. You realize that you're going to have to rethink how you imagine the controls—you're at the helm of a helicopter now—but you can handle it. So take evasive action and see what works!

The Flying R.A.T.s unleash a volley of laser fire at your chopper, but luckily they're low-level employees whose aim isn't that good, giving you more of a chance to fight back. Make a move!

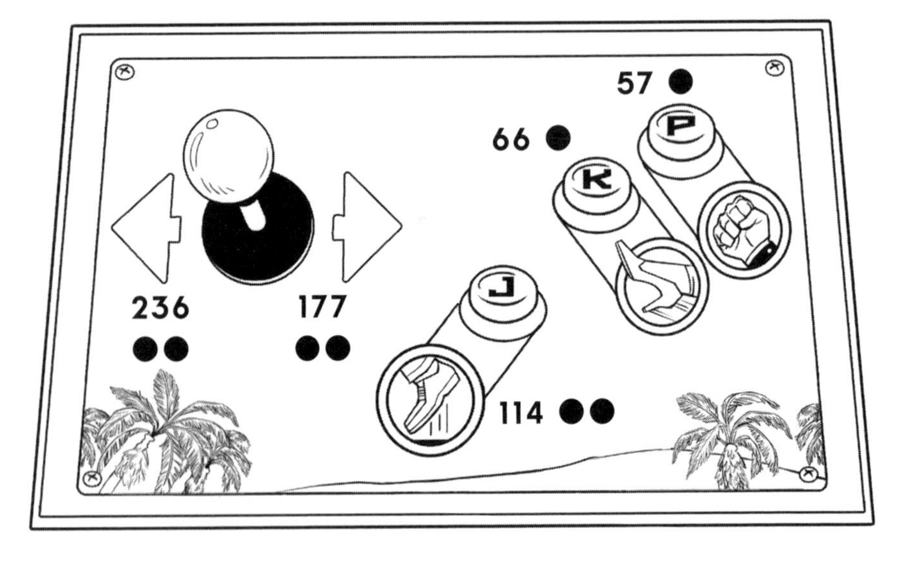

This is a game and you're going to win it, and no one ever beat a game by letting a bunch of upper-class "lawn jocks" bully their way to the high score. Grasping the controls of the Grass Yacht, you press down on the gas, and the engine revs.

"Oh, so you want to challenge the Rakes, do you? Ha ha ha ha ha! Ha ha! Ha! Well, have it your way. Kirk E., give this kid your rake, and then you and Kirk C. set up a perimeter!"

Kirk E. draws his rake and throws it toward you, and you catch it with one hand. Then he and the other

Kirk begin to circle their mowers around the lip of the bowl you're all in, creating a barrier between you and whatever escape you might want to make, leaving you and Kirk S. facing off in the bowl, riding lawn mower against riding lawn mower.

"The rules of Mow Bowl are simple," Kirk S. says, grabbing his rake and pointing it at you. "Two mowers enter, one mower leaves. Rakes are the only weapons allowed. Even a scrub like you should be able to understand that. Tallyho!"

And without any further ado, Kirk S. hits the gas on his riding lawn mower and heads directly toward you. What do you do?!

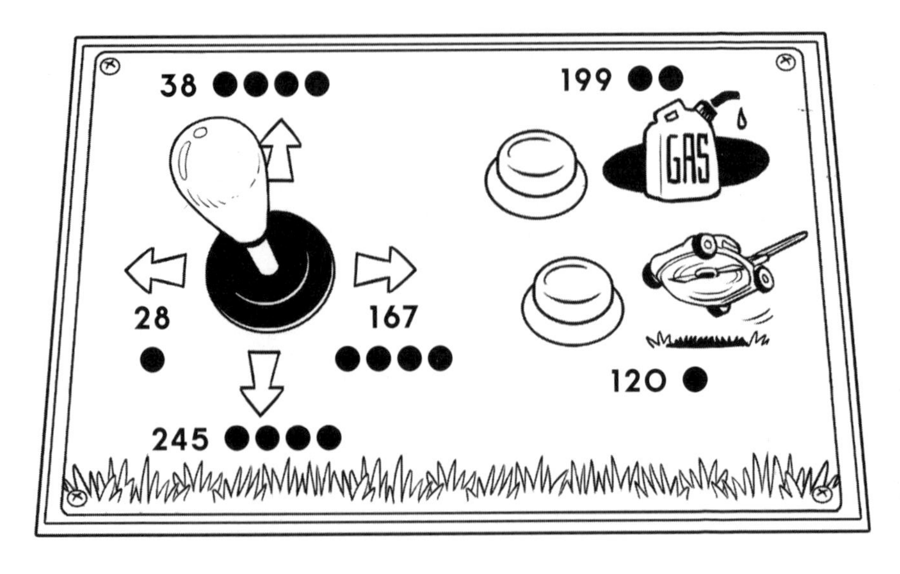

●●

There's two of them and there's two of you, and as a wise person once said, "It takes two to make a thing go right, it takes two to make it out of sight." Heeding that advice, you both slam your cybernetic fists together, and that action sends out a blast that flips both Dobermann Pincer and Pistolwhip end over elbow, cartwheeling directly into the King Snake Crawler! Their bodies blink a couple of times and disappear. Hey—two down, one to go!

Head to 74 ●

In a panic, you run directly toward the vicious topiary creature on your left, and too late you discover that its arms have thorns. Many, many thorns.

YOU ARE DEAD. CONTINUE: Y/N?

Y: Head to 129 ● N: Head to 248 ●●

●●●●

You meet the King Snake Crawler's charge with a double punch, denting its front end and halting its progress in the process! King Snake looks confused at the blow and dismayed at the damage you've caused. Yeah, that's how you do it!

Head to 216 ●●●●

●

You decide to swing yourself to the right, and the Topiasaurus moves slightly to the left, and you lose your footing, tumbling to the ground. You land on a small, soft bush without making much of a sound, and the monster doesn't seem to have noticed, which is fortunate for you. But now you're back where you started.

Head back to 110 ●●●

You nail the R.A.T. right in the chest with your foot, knocking her loose and sending her flailing down to the ocean below. These guys are TERRIBLE at their jobs!

Head to 206 ●●

●●●

The last of the R.A.T. henchmen taken care of, you look up at what should be the Exit sign on the gazebo. Instead, it reads "GO!" and is blinking rapidly. Knowing your video game cues, you smash through the double doors that lead to the parking lot outside. You're almost there! Across the lot, Captain Lu has the F.I.S.T.S. chopper running. He gives a thumbs-up, letting you

know that the helicopter's warmed up and ready for liftoff. You start to run toward your waiting ride, but halfway there your progress is stopped as someone emerges from between a parked midsize sedan and a minivan . . . another R.A.T. operative, a tall woman carrying both a laser pistol AND an electric whip? What?!

"Greetings, member of F.I.S.T.S.," she says, speaking in a very cool accent. "You may be tough and spoiling for a fight, but you shall go no further, for I am PISTOLWHIP, top operative of R.A.T. Come and get . . . your DOOM! Ha ha ha ha ha!"

You need to get to the chopper and go after your sweetheart, but "Pistolwhip" stands between you and getting into the air. What do you do?!

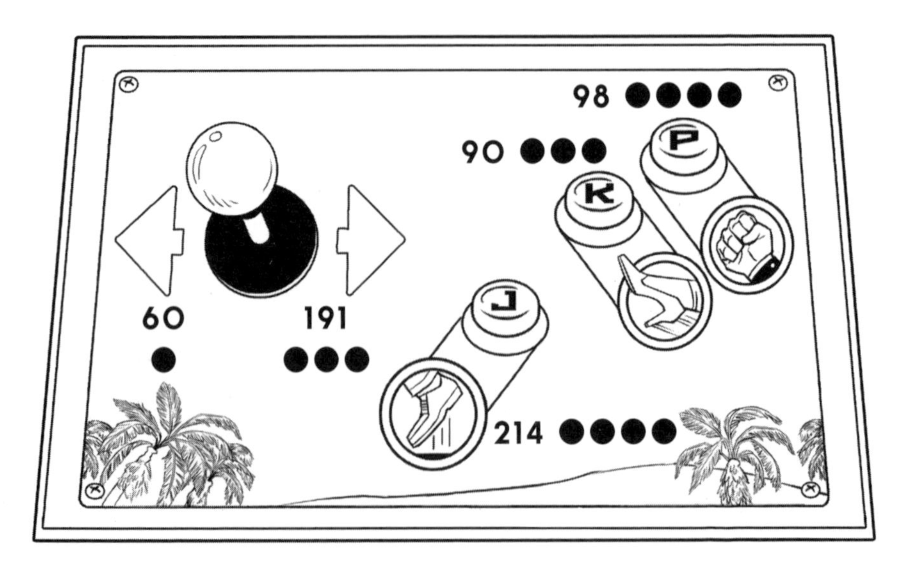

You walk up the steps that lead to the massive doors of the vast mansion. Reaching out, you grab a brass knocker fashioned in the shape of a circular ring of ivy and rap on the door once, twice, three times. The sound echoes inside, and then . . . the door slowly creaks open. Inside it's dark, and anyone else would be much more cautious before pushing ahead. You, however, have already faced vicious lawn-mowing street gangs and a giant mutant gopher on this fine summer day, so you walk right on in. What's the worst that could happen?

The inside of Vineland looks much like the outside; vines creep everywhere, over the floors and up the walls. What was once a fancy home now looks like a fancy greenhouse. Stepping cautiously over plant debris, you find yourself before another set of doors that lead to what you think might be a library. And behind them, you can hear something, and it sounds like . . . a baseball game on the radio?

Grasping the handles on the double doors, you pull them open and reveal what looks to be a massive and messy workshop and laboratory, full of strange lawn-care machines of all shapes and sizes, from ornate weed trimmers to bizarre lawn mowers to things you can't

even identify. The walls are lined with beautiful and elaborate blueprints and schematics. And in the middle of it all is a large worktable, at which sits an old man with a massive, wizardly beard. He's dressed in grass-stained overalls that also have a wizardly aspect to them, his attention so focused on the small transistor radio in front of him (and yes, it's broadcasting a baseball game, one between the Lawndon Darts and the Barbecue City Grills) that he doesn't notice for a moment that he has company. You clear your throat respectfully.

"Ah!" he says, looking at you as he turns off the radio. "Finally. Someone has made it this far. If you're here, that means you have the right stuff. Greetings—I am the ANCIENT GARDENER.

"I was once like you," says the Ancient Gardener, beckoning you closer. You approach the table, and as he speaks, you realize that the words from his mouth are wet and rank, like the smell of yard clippings. "I was the best yard kid in all of Lawndon. I saw a thousand yards, and I mowed them all. Other kids wanted to be like me, and so the competitions started, the rivalries began, and that's when 'MowTown' was born.

"But I turned my back on it. There was nothing new I could do down there in town. I could fix any mechanical problem on any model of lawn mower, from Mow-Luxes to Blade Barons, but the thrill was gone. So I took all the money I had saved from summer after summer, and I walked away, far up the hill, to this place, and bought the estate. It was here, in Vineland, where I could pursue my research into my new obsession: horticultural magic! I became a reclusive druid, a Wonka of root and grass. I made grass that would only grow to a specific height, flowers that would sing along to the radio, lawn chairs that could travel through space and time . . . Ah, such wonders I made with sorcery and soil!

"But my ambition became TOO great, and I sowed the seeds of my undoing when, like Frankenstein, I decided to make LIFE—the Topiasaurs, living creatures made of vine and leaf. You might have met some of them already if you found their lair in the garden below.

"But those were merely my first trial runs. I made another, one to rule over them, a king. But it was too powerful for me to control, and I have become too weak to battle it, so you must be the one to trim the creature down to size. You must battle TOPIASAURUS REX. But tell me: Do you have them? The Golden Hedge Clippers?"

If you've found the Golden Hedge Clippers, head to 3 ●

If you haven't found the Golden Hedge Clippers, head to 18 ●

●

You've come to a small semicircular area, a sort of bottle garden in the hedges. The vines and hedges that border the garden seem to be moving, though, ever so slightly. Weird. Besides that, there's nothing here, except for a vine-covered rectangular object directly ahead of you. What do you do?

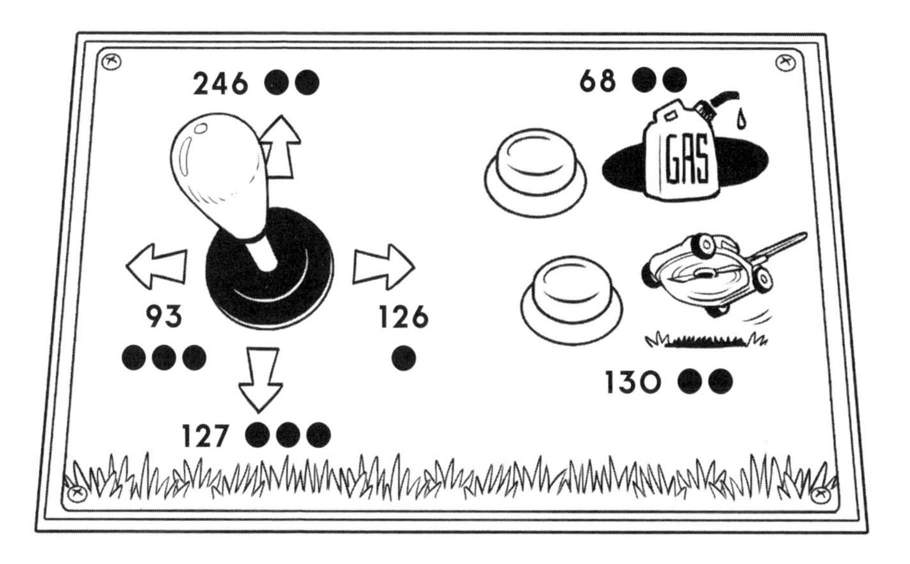

●●

Pulling back on the helicopter's controls slows the vehicle down and raises it up a little, allowing some laser fire to pass under you, but you need to be going FORWARD. Go!

Head back to 222 ●●●●

You slow down and pause in front of the brick. You stare at the brick. It stares at you. You are in a staring contest with a brick. There are probably more constructive ways to spend your time. Choose another move.

Head back to 204 ●●●

Pistolwhip moves forward, saying, "Face my pistol and my whip aga—" but you both move in quickly, interrupting her, taking her by surprise with a double uppercut, sending her flying back into the throne! She recovers, though, and bounces back up. That didn't quite do it. Try again.

Head back to 29 ●●●

●

You've landed on top of the King Snake Crawler, much to the consternation of King Snake, who shouts and fumes. "Get off!" he yells. "This isn't how this works!" Well, if that's the case, why don't you show him how it DOES work?

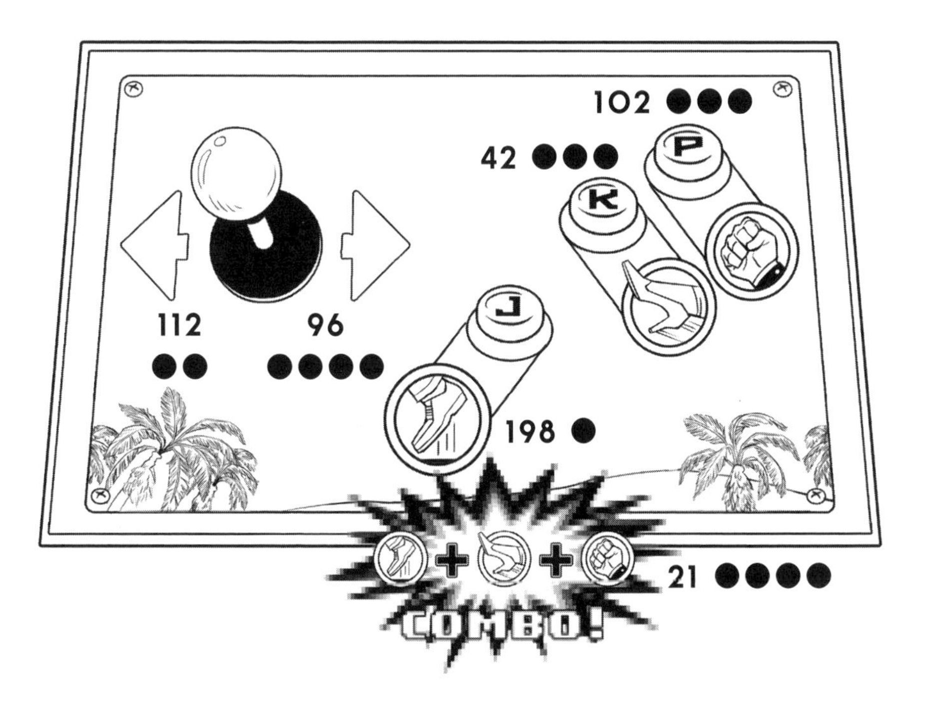

●●

You decide to explore the path to the left, and soon you're far down the twisty avenue, your way almost blocked many times by undergrowth. Sheesh, they need a gardener in this place! Soon, however, the path ends in a small, circular area.

Head to 235 ●

That way lies the wreckage of the chopper, forming a barrier for your fight. Choose another action.

Head back to 49 ●●●

You turn the Mow-Luxe to the right . . . and head directly toward the kid and their dog! The canine begins to bark at you furiously, straining at its leash . . . which then snaps! Joining Cutter, the angry dog begins to pursue you. You just can't win this morning, and now it's . . .

GAME OVER. CONTINUE: Y/N?

Y: Head to 103 ●●●● N: Head to 248 ●●

●

You shift the Grass Yacht into reverse and back into the Shed. The Mechanic waves his arms at you. "Whoa, whoa, whoa," he says, pointing at the exit. "The grass is that way." Move again!

Head back to 201 ●

●●

You hop up in your seat, but that's it. This move does nothing in the helicopter. Choose another move.

Head back to 203 ●●

The topiary creature on your left lunges toward you, so instinctively you move to your right, which sadly brings you into the arms of the creature on THAT side. Woe is you. Mow is you. Oh no is you.

YOU ARE DEAD. CONTINUE: Y/N?

Y: Head to 129 ● N: Head to 248 ●●

●●●●

You drive toward Murray, aiming directly at his stomach . . . and the impact of the Grass Yacht does nothing! It's like driving into a brick wall made of mutant gopher, and the Grass Yacht crumples like tinfoil. Murray roars his terrible mutant yawp and then opens his mouth wide to devour you and Kirk S. You always knew that lawn mowing was dangerous, and now . . .

YOU ARE DEAD. CONTINUE: Y/N?

Y: Head to 115 ●●●● N: Head to 248 ●●

●

You pull hard to the left, making the turn and heading down the cul-de-sac, at the end of which is a house almost overgrown with grass and weeds. That's it—it's the location on the map! In front of the house stands an old woman carrying a glass of lemonade on a tray. You've reached the location of your first job. Yes!

Head to 160 ●●●●

●●

Your missile streaks across the sky, headed directly toward your quarry . . . and connects! The last of the Flying R.A.T.s spirals down toward the sea below, landing in the water with what you're sure would be a very disturbing sound effect, could you hear it. Well done!

Head to 171 ●●●

Figuring that it's best to explore everything before you hit the spooky, vine-covered mansion, you decide to go along the path that leads to the right. Before long, you come to a dead end marked by a strange little enclosed garden.

Head to 47 ●●

Your kick makes a hollow sound against the floor of the chopper, doing absolutely nothing. Pilot, don't pout. Choose again.

Head back to 206 ●●

●

You jump up, and when you come down, you lose your footing on Topiasaurus Rex's shoulder (it IS moving, after all) and fall, the Golden Clippers slipping from your hands in the process. C'mon! This is not the way to win. You know it. Everybody knows it.

YOU ARE DEAD. CONTINUE: Y/N?

Y: Head to 3 ● N: Head to 248 ●●

●●

Using your collective momentum to your advantage, you both punch the giant Cyberanha simultaneously, so hard that you thoroughly annihilate the weird creature, turning its deep insides into its far outsides. You're covered in fish guts, but you're still going!

Head to 153 ●●●

●●●

You move away from the Topiasaurus's charging form, but not fast enough. The creature stomps on you, making you part of the soil. We all help to make the flowers grow, after all . . .

YOU ARE DEAD. CONTINUE: Y/N?

Y: Head to 129 ● N: Head to 248 ●●

One R.A.T. thug down, you advance into the large, glass-walled gazebo nearby, through which is the parking lot and the chopper. But as you run forward, you realize that you have many more R.A.T. rats to fight, for as you enter the gazebo (which is where your reception would have been held, and you wonder if you'll get your deposit back), you're surrounded by a crowd of thugs in the middle of the tastefully lit dance floor. They're in between you and the chopper, so . . . LET'S DANCE!

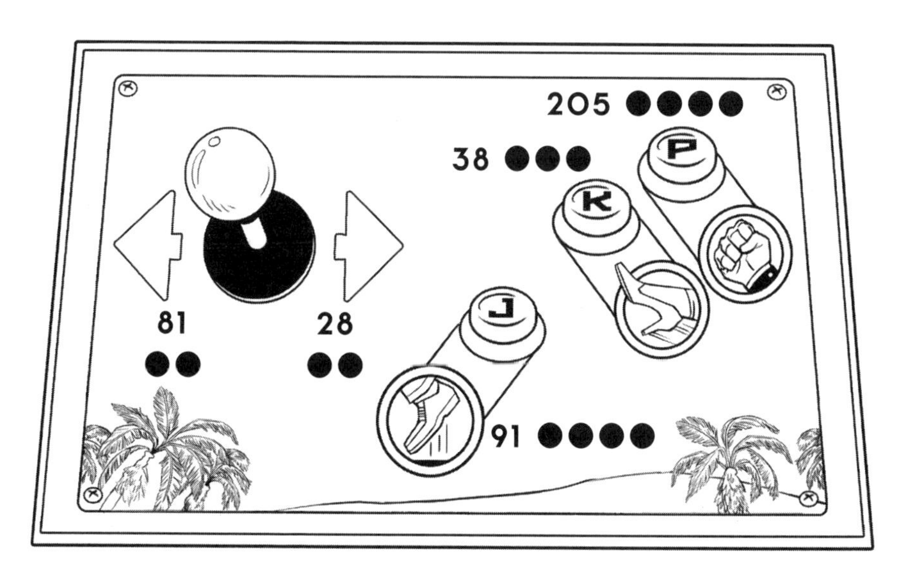

●

You push the Mow-Luxe straight on through, blowing past the intersection and farther into the neighborhood. But there's something strange about the new block you're on—at first it seems abnormally long, and then you notice that the houses on either side are actually repeating, refreshing themselves every few houses. And minutes later, when you haven't come to another intersection, it dawns on you that you might have encountered a glitch in the game, an endless loop where you're being chased forever by the Hedgelordz. That's . . . depressing. It also means that it's . . .

GAME OVER. CONTINUE: Y/N?

Y: Head to 55 ●● N: Head to 248 ●●

●●

You rapidly decelerate, hoping to avoid falling into Murray's sinkhole. The Grass Yacht's brakes and your reaction time aren't a great combination. You come to a stop on the lip of the chasm, and then the combined weight of you, Kirk S., and the lawn mower tips you over, and you fall into the darkness!

YOU ARE DEAD. CONTINUE: Y/N?

Y: Head to 24 ●●● N: Head to 248 ●●

●●●

You jump up as the King Snake Crawler aims its bulk at you, and you clear it entirely. It spins around 180 degrees and repeats its charge! Move again!

Head back to 74 ●

You put the Grass Yacht in reverse as Kirk S. heads toward you, and for a while he chases you as you backtrack. Finally, he stops, and you do the same.

"Hey, kid. You're in the Mow Bowl now—act like it and face me like a gardener!"

He puts his lawn mower in gear and accelerates toward you again. Choose another move!

Head back to 225 ●

●

You pull the controls back, hoping to stay outside of the doomsday device's blast range, but R.A.T. seems to believe in overkill, and the force of the explosion sends the chopper spinning out of control. That's it!

YOU ARE DEAD. CONTINUE: Y/N?

Y: Head to 203 ●● N: Head to 248 ●●

••

You move toward the viny object and kneel before it. The plants that cover it are dry and brittle, so you can tear them off easily. After a few moments you reveal what's underneath: an old, and very cold, metal ice chest. How long has it been here, and how can it STILL be so chilly? Throwing caution to the wind, you open the lid, hoping that it's not a trap . . .

. . . and reveal the contents inside: one lone can of Lawndon's Own Lemonade!

Figuring that this object could be important later, you stash the can in your back pocket and then walk quickly back down the path to return to the crossroads.

Head to 129 ●

You jump into the air, arcing toward the thug, but he swings his crowbar and connects with you like you were a slow and easy pitch in Little League baseball. Do video game characters have bones? If so, he just broke many of yours. Crowbars, right?

YOU ARE DEAD. CONTINUE: Y/N?

Y: Head to 146 ● N: Head to 248 ●●

●●●●

You move directly toward the head, so cautiously that it has time to turn and see you there. If enormous topiary creatures could smile, it would, because you're just close enough to be gobbled down like plant food, which is what happens.

YOU ARE DEAD. CONTINUE: Y/N?

Y: Head to 3 ● N: Head to 248 ●●

●

You both kick King Snake about the head, which is satisfying, but it's not the most effective finishing move. Do something . . . bigger when you choose again.

Head back to 56 ●●●

●●

Everything around you turns to fractionalized light and synthesizer sounds, overwhelming your senses until you don't know where you are anymore. You press your hands to your ears and close your eyes to shut it out, but you still feel as if you're trapped inside the cabinet of a particularly loud and garish video game. As suddenly as it started, it stops. Cautiously, you open your eyes . . .

. . . and see the Midnight Arcade. Still dim, still burbling with game activity, but empty. You call out "hello" a couple of times, but there's no answer. The only things inside are you and the games. You wander up and down the aisles, but there's no sign of the strange teenager who greeted you earlier.

Finally giving up, you make your way back to the arcade's front door, past the booth advertising the chess-playing chicken (and this time there actually IS a chicken in there, and it's currently taking its opponent's queen with its remaining knight), and finally back out onto the dark streets of Arcadia. But the strange thing is, they're not dark at all. When you push the door open, the bright light of morning hits your eyes! But . . . it can't be. There's no way you could have been inside all night, is there?

Climbing the stairs back to the level of the sidewalk, you ask the first passerby—a muscular man wearing a beautiful suit and a lucha libre mask that makes him look a little bit like a wolf—what day it is. His answer is impossible—it's the morning of the day you ditched school to go to the big city! You turn back to the storefront you just came from, but . . . it's not there! Instead, there's a butcher shop, complete with roasted ducks hanging in the window, and it looks like it's been there for years. Your mind reels, but you can't discount the evidence of your eyes. There isn't an arcade there, and from the looks of it, there never was.

You find yourself walking back to the Arcadia train station and descend into its depths. There's a train waiting there, about to depart, and you run for it, barely making it inside before the doors close. Soon, you're back in the main train station, a return trip that takes much less time than the trip getting there did, and from there you get on a commuter train out to your neighborhood, which deposits you blocks away from your school. You join the rest of the kids making their way to class, and as the morning bell rings, you realize that you haven't ditched school at all—you've somehow pulled a McFly and made it back in time!

Sitting at your desk, you gaze in wonder at your classmates. Something weird happened, but you aren't quite sure WHAT exactly, and they have no idea about the adventure you were just on. Well, the adventure you probably weren't on—for all you know, you might have to start dealing with an extreme sleepwalking problem. But that's a problem for another day, you tell yourself as your teacher's voice breaks your reverie. Class has begun, and you reach into your backpack to grab your textbook.

When you do, though, something at the bottom of the bag, amid the detritus of gum wrappers, earbud cords, and other junk, grabs your attention. Something gold, circular, and shiny. You grab it and hold it up and see that you're holding a coin. A token of some sort.

A token from the Midnight Arcade.

ABOUT THE AUTHOR

Known for the popular online role-playing game *Sword & Backpack*, Gabe Soria has written several books for Penguin Young Readers, including *Regular Show's Fakespeare in the Park* and Shovel Knight's *Digger's Diary*. He has written several comic books for DC Comics, including Batman '66. Gabe also collaborated with friend Dan Auerbach of the Black Keys on the *Murder Ballads* comic book. He lives in New Orleans, Louisiana.

ABOUT THE ILLUSTRATOR

Kendall Hale is a cartoonist from Wisconsin whose work has varied from animated character designs to commercial advertising. He has produced work for Nick Jr., Bento Box, Skippy Peanut Butter, and Sandman Studios. He has also taught classes at Brigham Young University. He currently lives in Los Angeles, California, with his pet rock, Rock.

This one's for A.P., because it's what you need to do—GS

PENGUIN WORKSHOP
An Imprint of Penguin Random House LLC, New York

Printed in the USA.

Visit us online at www.penguinrandomhouse.com.

Library of Congress Cataloging-in-Publication Data
is available upon request.

ISBN 9781524784331

10 9 8 7 6 5 4 3 2 1